BOSSY *Bride*
EMMA & JESSE
JA HUSS

Edited by RJ Locksley
Cover Design by JA Huss

BOSSY
Bride

EMMA & JESSE

NEW YORK TIMES BESTSELLING AUTHOR
ja HUSS

ABOUT THE BOOK

Jesse Boston is the man of my dreams. He's super hot, super rich, and super funny. He gets all my jokes, he treats me like a princess, and our love life is smokin' hot.

So I'm gonna marry him. I'm not real picky about how that happens and if my mother wants to have her say, fine. That's fine. She gave birth to three boys and just one girl. So I get it. She NEEDS a wedding.

But when she invites my childhood nemesis, KAREN, to plan our wedding AND be one of my bride's maids? Uh---no. It's not happening. Karen Krakken-Channing will not plan my wedding, will not be at my wedding, and she's certainly not going to be IN my wedding.

Luckily, my jet-butler, Miles, and my almost-husband get this great idea!

We're going to elope to Vegas on Christmas Eve eve, get hitched in the most ridiculous way possible, and then fly home in time for Christmas Eve dinner.

We've got it all figured out.

Nothing can go wrong.

We will have one simple wedding in like… a drive-through chapel, and call it good.

Take that, KAREN!

Bossy Bride features Jesse and Emma getting almost-hitched on a roller coaster, tricked into being the stars of a pirate show, jumping out of an airplane, and saying their vows in front of two huge Italian families who don't speak English. It's a rompy, whirlwind trip down a rabbit hole of "Fantasy" Vegas weddings planned by a man called "Fingers" and just when you think nothing else could go wrong—a mermaid descends from the ceiling.

CHAPTER ONE

JESSE

My first Bright Berry Beach holiday party.

Let me just set the scene for this insane group of cosmetics-crazy celebrators.

We have Mila Sanchez as Santa. That's right. Five-foot-tiny Mila dressed up, not as Mrs. Claus, but the actual Santa. She's got the fat suit. The black boots. The white beard. I'm talking the whole shebang. Plus, a red velvet sack filled with party favors.

Not gifts—I'll get to that in a minute. Party favors.

Mostly they are baked goods. Of the cannabis variety. But there are also tiny bottles of Dom Pérignon with a special Bright Berry Beach rose-gold foil label, and made-to-order Stefano Ricci silk ties with tiny crystal berry embellishments in both red and blue, and every now and then some lucky bastard pulls out a Breguet watch or a bright blue Tiffany box.

I just can't with Mila.

But I actually wouldn't mind one of those watches.

Too bad I pulled out a pot brownie. Emma ate it. Like in one gulp. Because I'm sober, so yeah. No pot brownies for me.

It's nine-thirty right now and everyone is pretty smashed on edibles, or champagne, or silk ties, or Breguet and Tiffany good luck.

I'm just watching this whole thing with a sort of detached fascination.

There is a little part of me that misses the old days. My yacht days. My party days. My sailing-the-world days filled with drugs, and drinking, and sex with strangers.

But it's a very small part of me.

I do enjoy watching Emma get wasted though. I've never seen her wasted. She's a fun drunk. Dancing and laughing, twirling and giggling. Her eyes are glassy and bright, her cheeks flushed all pink like she just had really hot sex.

I'm in the middle of formulating a plan to lure her up the escalators to her office so I can fuck her on her desk when she grabs the karaoke mic and starts singing *Jingle Bell Rock*. She looks at me and I get all tingly and warm when she winks and shakes her jingle bells.

God. Emma Dumas. One of a kind. And she's

mine. All mine.

We're getting married next spring and honestly, that's all I can think about. I know her bossy mom down in Key West is trying to take over the wedding plans and that's driving Emma up a wall, but I do not give one shit what the wedding looks like. I just want to pledge my undying love to her and then fuck her for a whole week straight in Tahiti.

Down, boy. Because I'm ready for that desk sex right now and she's currently the entertainment.

So. Back to the party.

Then we have Hannah. Tall and willowy nerd-glasses Hannah. She looks like a fucking runway model right now. If said runway model was dressed up like an alien elf. Which, I have to say, Hannah pulls off pretty well. Not many women can wear a bald cap, elf ears, and a tight silver minidress and still look hot.

Why is she dressed like an alien elf, you ask?

I'm not sure. It might have something to do with the AlienCon Christmas party down the street. I think she and what's-his-face the boyfriend just came from there because he's dressed up like a silver alien reindeer and he keeps saying, "Take me to your mascara," in a fake robot-slash-alien voice like this is the best joke ever.

Newsflash, what's-your-face. It's not. You're just drunk on edibles and your hot alien-elf girlfriend.

But the really interesting Bright Berry Beach partner here tonight is Natalie. She has two dates. She started the night with three, but one's a gynecologist and got called in for an emergency caesarian on triplets.

I'm pretty sure there's a joke in there somewhere— three men, three babies—but I can't seem to find it at the moment.

Anyway. Natalie currently has two dudes on her arms. She's wearing them like jewelry. And she's talking to my almost-sister-in-law, Brooke—who is now a full-time Bright Berry Beach independent cosmetic sales consultant for corporate parties, or... something?— and my actual, sorta-not-brother, Joey, and their two other partners, Wald and Huck, over by the punch bowl.

I'm reading their lips and formulating my own make-believe conversation as I watch this interaction go down...

Natalie to Brooke: *So, do you all sleep in the same bed?*

It starts out tame, but to the point.

Brooke to Natalie: *Oh, no. We take turns. There's just not a bed big enough to accommodate four sexy people such as ourselves at the same time.*

Natalie to Joey: *How's that work? Do you guys have a schedule? Like... you get Brooke on Monday and Thursdays?*

Joey to Natalie: Blank face with eye blinking.

Huck to Natalie: *I get Joey on Mondays and Thursdays.*

Natalie to Huck: Blank face with eye blinking.

Wald to Natalie: *He's kidding. He gets me on Mondays and Thursdays.*

Natalie's Boyfriend Number One: *Hahaha.* (as he elbows Natalie's Boyfriend Number Two)

Natalie's Boyfriend Number Two: Side-eyeing Number One.

Natalie to Wald: *Interesting.*

Natalie's Boyfriend Number One: *Very interesting. I'd like to hear more.*

Natalie's Boyfriend Number Two: *Who needs more pot brownies?*

Huck to Natalie: *Are you into swinging? Because we are.*

Natalie to Huck: *Hahaha.*

But then Number Two walks off and Joey starts kissing Brooke, and Huck grabs Joey's ass, and Wald...

Yeah. I'm out. I like Brooke, Wald, *and* Huck, but I really don't understand the logistics of their relationship. They cannot all fit in one bed. I mean, I guess they could make it work for some foursome sex, but sleeping? Where do they sleep? When Emma and I go over to visit them Joey calls Brooke's room his room. And Brook calls Joey's room her room. And both Huck and Wald have bedrooms on the lower level… so *where* do they sleep?

God, this bugs me. I need to know where they sleep!

I swing my gaze across the room to Johnny. Which—can I just say?—is hilarious. That he has to be here at this holiday party because Megan is now a full-time Bright Berry Beach employee. She's Hannah's new lab tech. Cooks up lipstick flavors or something.

Is it weird that the Boston brothers are now all connected to Bright Berry Beach? Is that too many B's? I'm not sure. Maybe it's not weird. But if Zach Boston ends up at next year's party, I will have to give this question some serious consideration.

Emma saunters over to me, still belting out *Jingle Bell Rock* and shaking her jingle bells, and I pause my people-watching to beam a smile at her.

So. Cute.

This girl is *so* cute.

Which reminds me. I still want to fuck her on her desk before we leave tonight. Preferably while the party is still in full swing with *I'm Dreaming of a White Christmas* subtly filtering up from the corporate office lobby…

But before I can grab Emma around the waist and whisk her off to the escalator that goes up to the executive offices, she's moved on. Singing to someone else.

I catch Johnny's eye from across the room and start heading that way. Megan is busy talking to what's-his-face near the dessert table, equally enthralled with the blinking red lights on his antlers and the red and green macaron tray in front of her, so Johnny is all alone.

He's not really social, so I figure I'm doing him a favor by coming by. But just as I open my mouth to say something, his phone buzzes in his pocket, and I pause.

I look at his pocket, then him.

He ignores the phone. Stares back at me.

"Aren't you going to get that?"

"I know who it is. So. No."

"Who is it?"

He sighs. It's one of those I'm-bored sighs. Or I'm-going-to-kill-you-now-if-you-keep-talking sighs. One or the other.

Have I mentioned I'm the charming one in the family?

I am.

"Fucking Alonzo."

"Alonzo." I say this not as a question, exactly. But it's definitely confusion. "Alonzo… as in my almost-brother-in-law?"

"The very one."

"Why is he calling you?"

"Do you think they're sneaky?"

"Who?"

"The fuckin' Dumas family."

"Sneaky how?"

"You know." He juts his chin at me. "Like us."

I shake my head and squint my eyes. "What?"

"Never mind."

"No, tell me."

"You're heading down there tomorrow, right?"

"Yup. Spending the whole week there. I can't wait." I really dig the Dumas family. Even though all Emma's brothers regularly size me up like they're about to jump my ass, I still like them. They're all just so... *likable*.

"Well..." Johnny looks side to side all craftily, like he's about to tell me a secret. "Set your alarm for three AM and look out your window at Jack and Silvia's house."

"Why?"

"No reason."

Now it's my turn to sigh. Ever since Johnny came back from the Caribbean last summer, he's been weirdly cagey, but not dangerously cagey. If that makes sense. And it does. To me, anyway. First of all, he really didn't come back with any information. Just this girl Megan. Who is some sort of scientist? But everything seemed to get better.

Better how?

Let me tell you how. Johnny and Megan moved up to the lake house. And he's no longer in charge of the money-making ceremony. Some guy called Chek is. Chek has this twelve-year-old daughter called Wendy who kinda creeps me out. I can't place my finger on it because she's kinda cute. And smart. And quiet. But she has this *look* she gives people when they're not paying attention.

This look reminds me of Johnny.

But then again, it reminds me of Chek too. So... maybe it's just genetics and I'm overreacting?

But here's the thing... I'm the sober one, right? I see things others miss because they're drinking beer, or eating pot brownies, or dressing up like alien elves and whatever. Sober is like a superpower. You see things. And of course, little creepy Wendy is sober too. So she has the same superpower.

Also, I'm pretty sure Johnny had something to do with Joey getting shared custody of his daughter, Maisy. Every other weekend. And Michael Conner didn't even put up a fight even though his family and all those other creepy families up on the Kane estate still have to pay their monthly... *contribution*.

Nothing really changed. And yet everything got

less *stressful.*

But that's twice I've used the word 'creepy' in less than five seconds of thinking time.

What's up with that?

Anyway, back to the point and my convo with Johnny. "What does Jack and Silvia's house have to do with Alonzo?"

Jack and Silvia are Emma's parents. *Super* cool people. Like… I cannot even tell you how much I love Jack and Silvia. They own a shitload of water adventure shops down on Key West and a whole block of bungalows two blocks from the ocean. So the whole Dumas clan lives on this same street and then they rent the others out to tourists when Emma and her Bright Berry Beach peeps aren't down for a visit.

Johnny holds up his hands like he's surrendering. "I'm just saying. Take a peek out the window at three AM and tell me what you see."

"OK, dude." I clap him on the back. He's not all there so sometimes it's just better to just agree with him and move on to another topic. "So what are you and Megan doing for the holidays? Got any big plans?"

I should know this. He *is* my brother. But I haven't spent a holiday with Johnny since… well, a long time ago. Probably over fifteen years ago. Long before our uncle and father died.

Johnny shoots me a confused look. "Holiday?"

"You know… Christmas?"

"Oh. I don't do church."

I laugh. I can't help it. "OK. Yeah. But you know, Christmas is about trees and presents."

"No, it's not."

"Dude, it so is. That's why we're here. At this party. There's a giant twenty-foot-tall tree in front of the window and a present machine near the exit."

Ah. That reminds me. The presents. Because Santa Mila's bag is only filled with favors. They have an honest-to-God present machine here. Everyone got a lanyard as they came into the party. It's got your name on it and everything. And you know what's cool about these lanyards? The name is on both sides. I like that. I totally hate when people are wearing lanyards and you're desperate to know their name, but it's flipped backwards, so you either have to pretend you know their name—this is often my problem. I can't remember anyone's name—or tell them to flip their fucking badge around so you can read it.

Anyway. When you leave the party, you scan your lanyard under the Santa Laser Machine (this is a trademarked brand invented by Alien Elf herself) and boom. You get an email that reveals your Bright Berry Beach present.

17

I'm so fucking excited about this, I can't even explain it. I don't need a damn thing in this life. Not one damn thing. I'm set now that Emma is in my life and my brothers and I are on speaking terms again. So I'm not even sure why I'm so excited about the Santa Machine. Might have something to do with Emma bragging about the present she got me. Even though I don't need it, everyone loves presents, right?

So I've been trying to figure out what she could possibly feel so confident about. A yacht? A Lamborghini? A house? What? What is she getting me?

But then... all my guesses are stupid. I don't even like Lamborghinis and Bright Berry Beach isn't buying me a yacht or a house.

But it could happen. Santa Mila is passing out mini-Dom Pérignon bottles like they're candy-canes.

"Christmas is about church." Johnny is adamant.

"Johnny. Brother. I hope to hell you got Megan a present for Christmas because if you didn't... you're just an asshole."

Johnny's gaze slams on over to Megan—who is helping herself to the dessert table like she's never seen red and green macarons before—and he makes a face. "Did you get Emma a present?"

"Of course! It's the best present ever, too. The. Best."

"What is it?"

"I'm not telling you."

"Jesse. I'm not gonna blow your surprise. I'm the secret-keeper, remember? Just tell me what it is."

"No. You'll steal it. Get your own brilliant Christmas present idea."

"You're a dick."

"You're a freak."

"You're a tabloid has-been."

"You're a tatted-up nobody with a dog named Jasper." Then I point at him. "See, now that would've been a great present. A puppy. Everyone wants a puppy for Christmas."

"Megan got me Jasper. And his name is cool."

"Well, there you go."

He makes a face at me. "There I go, what?"

"You have to one-up the puppy. That's how this works. And that's gonna be hard, you know? Like… puppy. Such a great present. I hope you brought your A-game."

I end the convo with Johnny on a high note, George Costanza-style, and mosey on over to the dessert table before Megan eats all the red and green macarons. She's currently got eight of them on her tiny plate.

Aside from Megan, I might be the only rich person

on the planet who adores a good macaron. And if Santa Mila's red-velvet party favor bag is any indication of her taste in macarons, they're gonna be better than good.

Megan is just stuffing a green one into her mouth when I come up next to her. Then she self-consciously places her hand in front of her face like this is gonna hide the fact that she's masticating an entire macaron.

"They're good, huh?" Then I pop one into my mouth to form a solidarity bond and not interrupt her good time. I'm coy like that.

She takes a moment to chew and swallow, then laughs. Not an uncomfortable laugh, or even an embarrassed laugh. Because she just nods her head and stuffs another one in. "Sorry," she says with her mouth full. "I'm pregnant. And these are the best macarons I've ever had."

I choke on my macaron. Almost spit it out. She slaps me on the back.

"Sorry." I cough. "I'm... did you say... pregnant?"

"Yup. I'm so fuckin' hungry. Like all the time. Excuse me. I need a whole tray of mini-wieners right now or I might starve to death."

And then she's off to chase down a waiter with a tray of mini-wieners.

I glance back at Johnny. Man. That dude didn't

waste any time.

But then... I sorta have this feeling like... who *is* this Megan girl?

Not sure. But I see Emma coming towards me, jingling her jingle bells, and I just add it to my list of things that make no sense about Johnny Boston and focus on what's important.

Fucking Emma Dumas on her huge CFO desk. Because Huck just started to karaoke *I'm Dreaming of a White Christmas.*

I take her hand and pull her towards the escalator. "Follow me. Because I'm about to rock your jingle bells."

CHAPTER TWO

EMMA

'Tipsy' might be the best word in the English language.

It implies so many good things. It's a cute word. Unlike 'drunk,' which just conjures up images of messy consequences.

'Tipsy,' on the other hand, is fun. It implies that you're rosy-cheeked and happy. It's a celebratory word. You got a promotion. You won a contest. Cake and other sweet desserts are involved. You're not drinking out of a bottle, you've got special champagne flutes. And there's music. Not ragey music, either. You're not drowning your sorrows, you're rejoicing.

And if your tipsiness comes with holiday songs, it's like winning the jackpot.

Jesse has my hand as we ride up the escalator to the executive offices. "Come on, Miss Bossy," he says as we reach the top and hook a sharp right to get in the next one. "I've got a special package for you to unwrap tonight."

"I'm coming." I giggle. Because I know what's on his mind. And I've got a little holiday party surprise for him as well. But as we rush over to the next escalator I look to my right and pull us to a stop.

Because down below… well. I love Christmas. Just love it. And we go all out at Bright Berry Beach.

Jesse is determined to get up to my office, but he spins back to me like a retracting yo-yo. "What are we doing?"

I let out a long sigh and look down at the executive lobby in all its lit-up glory. "I just want to memorize it for a moment."

I adore the Bright Berry Beach holiday party. I adore it so much that I'm usually sad the day after. It's a huge event for us and we spend months planning it and making sure that everyone has a good time. Everyone will go home tonight and thank their lucky stars that they work for us. They will be tipsy too. And they will have party favors, and a bonus, and they will have spent the last several hours with people they care about.

We're not real family here. In a few days most of them will be with their real family. But we are *a* family.

24

The kind of family you choose.

We use the top twenty floors of our building for the company. Most of them are just floors and floors of offices, and cubicles, and the research and development labs.

But up here—on the top five floors of the Bright Berry Beach building—it's… kind of magical.

Especially during the holidays.

The Bright Berry Beach executive lobby is five stories tall and there are two massive walls of windows that showcase the city lights outside. The tree is twenty feet tall at least, and it takes a whole team of people an entire week to decorate it. The theme is pink and gold. So very, *very* Bright Berry Beach.

Huck is singing *I'm Dreaming of a White Christmas* and when I squint my eyes, I can see that it's actually snowing outside.

Everyone is dressed up. Some of them are wearing costumes, like Hannah and her boyfriend—there are lots of sexy elves. And some of them are conservative, opting instead for the little black or gold dress. Most of the men are in tuxes. I glance over my shoulder at Jesse, who has his arms around my middle now, his chest pressing up against my back. He's in a tux. But it's not his tux I see. It's his eyes. Such beautiful, thoughtful, sexy eyes.

I will never get tired of gazing into them.

"I love you," I say.

He kisses my cheek. "Miss Dumas, I didn't even know what love was until I met you."

I turn around, my hands automatically slipping up to his shoulders and then around his neck. I play with the longer strands of brown-blond hair that almost touch the top of his collar. And when I look right into his eyes and see myself looking back, I don't need to be tipsy to feel lightheaded and dizzy.

He does that to me all on his own.

"I can't wait to marry you, Mr. Boston. I wish we could do it right now. Right here, in front of all these people and that huge tree lit up in pink and gold."

He reaches up for my left hand and brings it into his lips. Kisses my knuckles gently. "Emma, my life has been a celebration from the moment you bought me at a bachelor auction." And then he turns me around, places both of my hands on the brushed metal railing, and leans forward.

"Attention!" he yells down to the crowd. "Can I have your attention, please?"

People look up. Huck stops singing. The music stops.

"I just need a moment of your time. I just need to shout it out. I love this woman! I love Emma Dumas and next spring I'm going to marry her!"

People laugh and cheer. Shout up encouragement. Some of them are yelling for more.

But Jesse is suddenly in motion. He's got my hand and he's pulling me over towards the next escalator.

But he doesn't get on. Instead he whisks me into his arms and starts running up the escalator.

Everyone down below knows what we're up to now, thank you very much, Mr. Boston, because they are whistling and cheering.

And I don't even care.

Let them know.

Let the whole world know.

I am in love with this man.

When we reach the top, he sets me back on my feet and tugs me along hurriedly towards my corner office. And then we're rushing through the door. Huck is singing again. The low hum of conversation fills in the background.

He turns me around and presses his body up against mine, walking me backwards until I reach the hard edge of my huge wooden desk. Then his hands reach behind my thighs and he lifts me, and the hem of my pink skirt, up and sets me on top of it.

I'm already unbuckling his belt, my fingers desperate for access. Not even caring that the door to my office is wide open.

He's unbuttoning my pink chiffon blouse and halfway down he gives up and just pulls it out of my skirt. But his hands are already inside it, squeezing my breasts and then yanking my strapless bra down so he can play with my nipples.

I don't love Jesse Boston just for his sexual prowess, but his skill certainly doesn't hurt.

Especially when, just as my hands have his pants open and are reaching inside to wrap around his cock, he presses forward, forcing me to lie back on the desk.

And then my legs are bending at the knees with the urging of his hands, and he's opening them up. His fingers slip between them, right past my carefully coordinated pink-lace panties, and penetrate me.

I close my eyes with a moan, but then open them again immediately. I want to see him. I want to see every moment with him. The tipsy inside me is suddenly gone. There is no alcohol or edible-induced lightheadedness.

Just a dizzying moment of passion and happiness. Totally organic.

But there's also a moment of vulnerability here.

I am spread out before him and his gaze wanders over my body as he continues to finger my pussy, and I feel… exposed.

But not in a bad way.

No. In the *best* way.

I want him to see me. All of me. The way I want to see all of him.

I bite my lip as he backs off just enough to close my legs, pull my panties down, and then open them right back up. A moment later he's bending down, his mouth open. And then…

"Ahhhhh, *God*." I grip his hair as he licks me.

It's a moment of pure bliss. Every time. I don't care how often he eats me out like this, every single time his tongue flicks against my sweet spot, I die a little with ecstasy.

I don't need to guide his head or give him pointers, but my fingers play with his hair and move his head around anyway. My hips begin to squirm as he pushes my legs up to my breasts, spreading me open.

I will not come like this.

I will not come like this.

I say it like a mantra. I want to save all the glory of my release up for when he enters me for real. When his hard, thick cock is fully inside me. Filling me up like nothing else in the world can.

But every time, I lose. His mouth is just *that* good. His lips are just *that* soft. His tongue is just *that* talented.

He laughs when my back bucks up off the desk.

And then he's encouraging me with words as he slips his fingers inside me.

I can't help it.

I come.

But before I'm done, he's inside me for real. Leaning over my body as he thrusts forward. I laugh and hug him tight against my body.

Then… a surprise. He lifts me up, grabs my ass and presses me to his hips, and carries me around the desk. I wrap my legs around his waist to keep him inside me, and then he sits on my large, soft, executive leather chair. The momentum sends the chair rolling backwards until it hits the wall of windows behind my desk. My knees settle on either side of his thighs and I begin to rock up and down as we press our foreheads into each other.

It's the most perfect moment ever.

We fuck slowly. It's a tender I-love-you lovemaking. Bathed in the glow of city lights and a soundtrack of happiness floating through my open office door from the party down below.

A duet of *Baby, It's Cold Outside.*

But it's not cold up here.

Up here… it's nothing but hot.

I don't fix my hair when we're done and pulling ourselves back together. And neither does he. We are a tousled mess of afterglow.

It's like we want them all to know what we did. Not that there's any doubt in anyone's mind at the party. They know.

I just want to make sure.

I want to show this man off to the entire fucking world and say, *He's mine*!

Jesse is standing at the top of the escalator. He squeezes my hand as he looks down at the people below. Then he side-eyes me in that coy, I'm-Jesse-Boston way he has, and says, "You're mine."

Ha.

We don't rush back down the escalator. We stand there like the king and queen of Bright Berry Beach. People notice us return. They notice with sly glances and whispered giggles behind hands over their mouths. But it's a good-natured kind of attention.

There is no doubt in anyone's mind that we are in love.

We separate then. Jesse heads off towards his brothers and their dates and I mingle a little, smiling and wishing our employees a happy holiday as I make my way over to my girls.

Hannah and Darrel are doing one of those corny,

intertwined-arm champagne toasts. You know, the one where you loop your arm around his and then drink your bubbly as a team. They are sorta cute in their own nerdy way.

Mila and her husband, Diego, slow-dance like the married couple they are. They've been together for almost a dozen years now, so their secret office-desk trysts at the holiday party are probably behind them. But I remember when they used to sneak away for secret sexy times.

Natalie and her two dates. I don't remember their names. She might not even have told me their names. Natalie is a woman who likes to keep her options open. But I'm sure, if she hasn't fucked them both in some out-of-the-way empty office, she will before the night is over.

I linger at the punch bowl and just... enjoy our success.

Because that's what this holiday party was always about. A way to bask in the glory of how we did it. We made it. We pulled ourselves up, and changed the future of our families. And yeah, there was a lot of hard work involved. But one night of every year we stop to say thanks and to celebrate with the people who decided to take this ride with us.

Then it's late. After midnight. Mila steps up to the microphone to make her annual holiday speech. It's filled with gratitude. She can be humble when she wants to, and this is her humble speech.

All faces go solemn as she begins to express our collective thanks. Then everyone is smiling and clapping when she calls people out by name, expressly thanking them for their Bright Berry Beach contributions.

And then Hannah takes over and invites everyone to visit the Santa Machine on their way out.

Everyone gets a cash bonus that will be automatically deposited into their bank accounts once they scan their lanyard. But everyone gets a personal present too. Sometimes they are just earrings, if that employee is an earring lover. Or a nice pair of cashmere gloves. But sometimes they are scholarships to the college their kid wants to go to next year. Or a new car, if theirs came to a sudden demise recently and they are now forced to take the bus to work.

When everyone gets back from the holiday break in the new year a new page on the employee website will pop up and there will be a form you can fill out. A form asking for a gift for a friend. You're not allowed to ask for your own gift. Someone has to do that for you. And if you're crazy and say, 'I'd like Bright Berry Beach to pay off my co-worker's house,' we look very closely at the reason why before we do something that extravagant.

But we don't ever say no outright to anything. Not if someone needs help.

Do we buy their loyalty? Or do we earn it?

It's actually not that hard to know. If someone is here just to get the gift from the Santa Machine, they are in for a sad reality check. All gifts are based on need.

Some years you get earrings or gloves, but when you need it—when you really, *really* need it—we're there to send that kid to college or pay that mortgage off.

The party begins to wind down as people pass their lanyards under the Santa Machine laser and say their goodbyes and well-wishes.

Mila, Hannah, Natalie, and I always meet in the executive conference room while this is all happening so we can take a moment to appreciate each other and revel in the success of the past year.

Sometimes there are more failures than successes, but we always try to concentrate on the positives. Some years we pay for this extravagant party out of our own pockets.

But not this year. This was a great year.

"Whew!" Hanna practically slides into one of the oversized leather conference table chairs, scooting backwards so she can kick her alien-elf feet up onto the brushed metal table. "Those edibles were the best idea ever!"

"They so were," Mila exclaims, slumping down into her own chair. "I had three." She wobbles a little and the chair rocks backwards a little too far, so she has to lean forward and catch herself. But she's smiling like a Cheshire cat in a Santa suit. Her beard is gone and so is the stuffing that made her look like a plump apple, so her suit is loose and the belt is missing. She toes off her black boots and puts her candy-cane-socked feet up on the table too.

Natalie is still drinking, a full flute of bubbly Dom in her hand as she leans against the wall with a sigh. "Well," she says, looking at me. "Tell us, Ems. How did we do this year?"

I'm in charge of our bonuses. That's why we meet after the party.

"Exceptionally." I beam. "I'm not sure what was so different about this year, but… ladies. We *killed* it."

"What's the number?" Hannah asks. "I need to hear it out loud!"

I take a breath. Because it's a *big* number. "Twenty-four point three million."

There's silence as that number sinks in. It's almost double the bonus of our best year ever.

"Wow," Mila exclaims. "Just… like… wow. I had no idea."

"Me either," Natalie says.

"OK. So that means we have a lot of work to do right now." I turn to the laptop on the conference table and bring up the list. "Who will it be?"

Everyone scans the list. And then the room becomes thoughtful.

"I think the lion's share should go to the Children's Hospital," Mila says.

"Agreed," we all chant in response.

"And then I'd like a big chunk to go to the inner-city arts and music program," Natalie says.

"And don't forget the new science and technology charter school," Hannah adds.

I take notes as we divvy up our annual bonuses. We have seventy-three candidates on our giving list this year. All of them needy. All of them deserving. And it will take time to make sure they all get their share of the money.

The Boston brothers are matching our charitable gifts this year. So there's actually almost fifty million dollars to divvy up tonight and that's gonna take a while.

36

For a moment I worry that Jesse will be bored as he waits out in the lobby with all our partners and guests. But I can see him through the glass walls of the conference room.

He and his brothers and their dates are lounging on the leather couches in front of the giant tree. Hannah's Darrel is out there talking to Diego and Natalie's boyfriends.

Every once in a while, one of them glances at us.

But they just nod and smile.

Do your thing, those smiles say.

Because they know that this meeting is the real meaning of the season.

CHAPTER THREE

JESSE

"Did I ever tell you about that little girl in the hazmat suit?"

Joey and Huck are laughing about something. Megan and Brooke have their heads together scheming about who knows what. And Wald is leaning into me, asking where I got my tie, when this comes out of Johnny's mouth.

"What?" we all say, stopping all our conversations mid-sentence.

He's drunk. Hell, everyone but me is drunk.

"The girl in the suit," Johnny insists. "The one I left in the middle of the ocean."

"What?" This time we all laugh out the word.

"Oh. My. God. *What?*" Johnny says, as he looks at Megan. We all look at Megan. She's making one of those slicing motions across her throat, which is the dead giveaway that Johnny is about to tell a true story.

I glance at Joey and find him looking back at me with raised eyebrows. That look says, *What's he talking about?*

I have no clue what Johnny's going on about. But I can't wait to hear it. And he doesn't disappoint. Suddenly we're all on a superyacht in the middle of the Caribbean with some dude named Logan and his crew of henchmen.

"Umm... OK. Maybe we should table this for another night, Johnny?" That's Megan. Apparently, she was here for this little adventure.

"No, no, no." Johnny laughs. "They gotta hear about the little girl. She was stealing biological samples from a secret lab on this island and..."

The whole thing derails from there. There's a helicopter story, and Megan chained in a dungeon, and something about rats who live forever.

At first we're all like, *Holy shit. What the hell is he talking about?*

But by the time he gets to the fountain-of-youth rats, we've all gone back to our respective conversations. He's totally making this shit up.

"Custom-made," I tell Wald.

"What?" He's still half listening to crazy Johnny.

"The tie," I say. "It was custom-made by this little

Italian tailor just outside of Vatican City. It's not really mine, it was my father's tie. But I was looking for something red to wear tonight and this just popped out at me. So… where do you sleep?"

"What?" he says again, only this time it's a laugh.

"You know." I nod my head at Joey and Huck. "Like… do you guys have a custom bed? How does this work?"

"We take turns," he says, sipping from a glass of water.

"No shit." I knew it. "Is there like… a schedule? And do any of you get jealous?" I know this is prying, that Joey's sex life is none of my business, but I can't help it. I'm… intrigued.

"Jealous?" Wald is still confused. "Um… well. No. I don't think so. I mean, I love them all equally."

"Equally? Like… totally equally?"

"Yup. I don't care which one of them I sleep with. It's all pretty nice. So we just… fall into whichever bed we feel like it, I guess. Normally I sleep with Brooke."

"You do?"

"Yeah. Joey likes to sleep alone. But sometimes he sleeps with Brooke too. Huck sleeps with me most nights."

I have to admit—this is a crazy arrangement. But it's all kind of exciting too.

"Nice," I say.

"Who do you sleep with?" Wald deadpans.

I laugh. "Emma. Just Emma."

"Well, that's… lovely." He says it like he feels sorry for me. Like I have no idea how fun his haphazard sleeping arrangements are and he's the luckiest guy in the world.

I can't really disagree with that, but I'm more than satisfied with just one sleeping partner.

"And then she looks me dead in the eye and says, 'I'm going on my first date next weekend and I'm kind of excited about it.'"

Only Megan laughs. She's the only one still paying attention to Johnny.

But then Johnny is laughing too, and I have to stop listening to Wald go on about his plural arrangement to enjoy that look for a moment.

Johnny Boston. *Laughing.*

My brother. Happy.

I love it.

This makes me think about my own happiness. And when I glance at the woman responsible for that new feeling on the other side of the glass-walled conference room, I find her looking back at me.

I point my finger at her and she beams a smile at me, then turns back to her charitable giving tasks and

I look around the room.

One year ago. What the hell was I doing last Christmas?

I have no clue what I was actually doing on this particular day one year ago, but last Christmas Eve Zach and I were in the Bossy Building on my floor watching reruns of *It's a Wonderful Life*. I was thinking I could relate to that dude, but looking back on it now, I can see I was wrong. Jimmy Stewart's character—I forget his name in the movie—he was the glue in his community. He sacrificed his own happiness and future for the good of everyone.

I glance at Johnny—who is still talking about this psycho little girl with Megan—and realize… it was him, actually. Johnny was the one who sacrificed his future for the rest of us.

I kinda respect the dude for that. I might not know him well, but I respect him. And I hope this Megan girl is the real deal.

Which reminds me… she told me she was pregnant.

"So… uh… hey," I say, directing my words at Johnny. He stops talking and looks at me. "You got any big news you want to share with us, John?"

Megan smiles big. But Johnny just looks confused.

"You know," I say, winking. "The baby?"

And then… in that moment… I see him.

I see *Johnny*. Maybe for the first time ever.

My brother. My big brother. My big, badass, dangerous,   I-will-kill-you-if-you-look-at-me-wrong brother.

His whole face changes. Like right before my eyes. And then he glances up at Megan and I swear to God, there's a tear in his drunk fucking eye.

"No," he says.

"Yup." Megan beams.

"Really?"

"Oh, shit," I say. "I didn't know it was a secret."

But they give no fucks about me. Johnny pulls Megan into his lap and hugs her tight. And I don't know. It's weird, for a moment. Like there's something deeper going on here than just the good news of a baby.

But then everyone is congratulating them, and the Bright Berry Beach men come over to see what's going on, and that feeling drifts away as this new kind of happiness washes over us.

Suddenly everyone is standing, me included. And we're all slapping Johnny on the back, and the girls are hovering around Megan, and then Emma is there. Emma and Natalie. Mila and Hannah.

Everyone is here.

All the important people in our new lives. Together.

"What's going on?" Emma says, sliding her hand into mine.

"Johnny and Megan are having a baby."

"Wow. Holy shit." And then she's in on it too.

I look up the giant Christmas tree backlit by the city lights and the trappings of a fantastic night all around us, then wonder if it's real. Wonder, *How the hell did I go from being a lonely, despised outcast to the inner circle of this fantastic group of people in just one year?*

Half a year, really. Because Emma and I have only been reconnected since last summer.

Somehow, I find myself in front of the Santa Machine, looking down at it. It's like a legit robot Santa. Like one of those wide, circular fake-security bots that the city started putting in the parks last year. But he's got a beard, and bushy eyebrows. And to scan your lanyard you pass it through his mouth.

I chuckle just thinking about the craziness of this idea. And the wacko imagination of Alien Elf and her nerdy boyfriend.

"Did you scan yours?"

I turn to see Emma coming up next to me. "Not yet."

"Well, good. Because you're not on the list,

buddy."

"What do you mean?"

She leans up and kisses me on the mouth, then whispers, "You're not an employee, Jesse. You have to wait until Christmas morning like everyone else. Now, come on. Take me home. I just spent fifty million dollars and I'm exhausted."

We say our goodbyes, grab our coats, and head down to the garage where Emma's Huracán is waiting.

I get to drive home. One of the perks of being sober.

But I'm still drunk. I'm drunk on her.

My Emma.

And when we get back to our apartment, we drop the car off with the valet and I hold her hand all the way up to the penthouse.

We share this place now. It's ours.

But when we walk inside, I glance at the wall of windows just before Emma flicks on the lights, and see the Bossy. All lit up for Christmas in a pattern of gold that makes it look like a beacon.

Is someone living on my floor now? Did Chek get all our stuff? Will I ever go back there? Or is that place a part of my past now?

"Are you coming?"

I turn and look at Emma. Her head is tilted to the

side a little, like she has a question for me.

"No," I say, walking over to her and taking her hand. Then I look down into her eyes and say, "I'm already here."

I have the craziest dream.

Like seriously, insane dream.

We're all there. All of us. Johnny and Megan. Joey, and Huck, and Wald, and Brooke. Emma and me. Mila and Diego. Hannah and what's-his-face. Natalie and the two guys from the party, even though those guys are just her current flavor of the month and don't really belong. Dreams are weird like that.

For some reason we're at the Kane estate. Charlotte is there too, even though Johnny told us that she's dead. I don't know why we're up at the Kane estate. I have only been up there once, and that was recent. I rode up with Joey to pick up Maisy for one of his father weekends when Huck and Wald were out of town on business and Brooke was at work.

It was a nice drive up, I guess. But then the guard at the gate said he knew me. There was this weird conversation with him. We went to school together. I swear to God, I have no recollection of that dude.

47

But anyway. He was there. The guard. And we were at the Kane estate. All of us.

There was some kind of weird ceremony. Not the money-making one that Joey described after that weird shit-show went down earlier in the year, but something else.

A wedding, I think it was.

Except we were *all* getting married. Only not to each other. Like, I wasn't marrying Emma, and Johnny wasn't marrying Megan, and Joey and the guys weren't marrying Brooke.

We were all marrying something else.

The Way, I think.

I think it was a dream about being married to the Way.

A subconscious message that this happiness we've found is just an illusion.

That we'll never break free.

I wake up in the middle of the night sweating and throw the covers off me. Emma is on her stomach, snoring softly, the light from the city outside illuminating her dark hair with bits of gold and red.

And I don't know, but… I can't shake this feeling

that the great time we just had at the holiday party is just an illusion.

I swing my legs out of bed, walk down the hallway, and open the door of the fridge. White light spills out past the door and I just stare into it. And come to a realization.

I need to marry her. Like now. Like *now*.

I don't want to wait until spring.

But I can't marry her now. We've got plans. Hell, in a few hours we'll be on the jet to Key West and by dinner tomorrow night we'll be completely wrapped up in Christmas preparations.

"It's fine," I tell myself, grabbing a bottle of water and closing the door. It was just a dream. Everything is going great. Johnny is having a baby, for fuck's sake. I'm gonna be an uncle again. Joey and his partners are all happy and satisfied. Maisy comes every other weekend to spend time with them.

Hell, I even have a fucking client. First fucking client in years. Some young teenager who wants to learn how to race yachts. He's not from a big important family, and I'm not taking money for it, but still. This kid… he's good. He reminds me of myself at that age. And I could be a part of his rise. A huge part.

Everything is good. Everything is perfect. And next spring Emma and I will have the perfect wedding and it will only get better.

Even Zach is doing things. I'm not really sure what, but he's living down on Key West and working with Emma's brother, Luke, on some boat.

We made it.

We got out.

We gave away fifty million dollars to charity last night.

But my eyes wander back to the Bossy Building across town. It's like a siren song calling me back.

"Fuck." The sound of my own voice startles me out of the lingering dream-state. "Jesus Christ, Jesse. Pull yourself together. It's just a stupid building."

I uncap the water, drink it down, cap it back up, and then go back to bed.

Emma turns over when I get in under the covers, her hands instinctively wrapping around my upper arm as she snuggles up to my chest.

I push the weird dream away. I push all the anxiety away and concentrate on what I want instead of what I think I deserve.

Because deep down I want Emma, but I don't think I *deserve* Emma.

And I do.

Dammit, I do. She was the first girl who ever found her way past the thick, cynical, drugged-up walls around my heart. And she never left. She's been in there, inside me, for thirteen years.

It's our time now.

So I think about that instead.

I think about sleeping with her every night for the rest of my life.

I think about Saturday night dinners with her family. I think about that whole street of cottages the Dumas family owns and how her mother already calls the blue one the Emma and Jesse house. How we will spend our lives down there with them. And maybe my brothers and their partners will have their own houses too.

One will be called the Joey, Huck, Wald, and Brooke house. And one will be called the Johnny and Megan house. Alonzo will be my friend and we'll go fishing with his father every summer and catch giant swordfish. And we'll go diving with Tony, and boating with Luke.

Maisy will be there, learning to dive, and swim, and fish, and sail, and then Johnny's new baby. One day, Emma and I will have our own crew. We'll sail the world with them, and teach them how to read the stars in the sky, and we'll go places. Special, faraway tropical places you can only get to by boat.

And one day, years and years from now, we'll

forget.

We'll forget all about the Way. And the Bossy. And the Kane estate and their missing, dead daughter.

We'll forget that my father and uncle were killed. We'll forget all the bad things and only remember the good ones.

That's how I fall asleep.

Forgetting.

But I wake up in the morning remembering everything. The dream. The fear. The Bossy.

And that fucking building is still staring at me from across the city when I look out the window.

"What are you doing, Jesse?" Emma is rushing around the penthouse like a crazy person, trying to pack up everything we'll need for a week in the Keys. "Did you call the car service?"

"Yup," I say, shaking myself out of the lingering bad dream. "And the jet is fueled and waiting for us. My man Miles is baking up those Barbie and Ken mini-rolls as we speak."

Emma is rushing past me with an armful of clothes that require a garment bag for travel when she practically skids to a stop, then places one hand on my cheek, gazes affectionately—I might even go so far as to say passionately—into my eyes, and beams a smile at me that could power space rockets and light up the solar system.

Then she kisses me on the lips, pats my cheek, and says, "You can eat the man-sized ones if you must. I'm just saying, the little ones taste better."

They taste the same. They are scrumptious little bits of creamy sugar syrup and layers of doughy cinnamon that literally fuckin' melt in your mouth. No chewing necessary. It makes no difference what size they are.

But I don't want the man-sized ones. The mini ones remind me of our first date. And that... that was probably the best day of my life. I'm not even sure our wedding day could top first-date day, that's how much fun I had on our first date.

"What's wrong with you?" Emma asks.

"What do you mean?"

"You've been acting weird all morning."

"Have not."

"You so have. Are you disappointed that you didn't get a Santa Machine present?"

I chuckle. "Well... maybe a little. But"—I grab her by the waist just as she tries to slip away and finish packing—"you're all the present I need. And anyway, we'll be in Key West in a few hours and I can forget all about that stupid building."

She cocks her head at me. "What?"

"Nothing. Never mind. Come on. Let's finish packing. We're officially on vacation. No more serious thoughts until the new year forces us back to reality. For the next nine days it's nothing but the ocean, and sandy toes, and your crazy mother and her wedding plans."

"Do not encourage her, Jesse. I'm telling you, if we give in an inch, she'll take over the whole wedding. And the next thing you know we'll be walking down an aisle called Dumas Street."

Dumas Street is what the family affectionately calls their little cul-de-sac of cottages. "I don't know. I think I could live with that."

"Don't!" Emma points to me, face serious. "We only get one wedding, Mr. Boston. I want it my way."

I put my hands up, surrendering. "Of course. It's your day and the bossy bride always gets her way. But"—I point to my eyebrows as I waggle them—"it's not your day yet."

Then I tackle her to the couch.

CHAPTER FOUR

I go crashing backwards, clothes flying off to the side, and internally I'm fuming. Because we're on a schedule here. The car is probably downstairs, the jet is on the tarmac, and neither of us are packed or even dressed. My hair and makeup are done, but I'm still wearing my pink satin dressing robe. And Jesse hasn't even taken a shower yet. He's walking around in his red pajama pants and no shirt, his hair all tousled and messy, his jaw still scratchy, and—

"Oooo!" I squeal. Because he's kissing me and his hands have found their way inside my robe. They're cold and wandering all over my breasts.

He pulls my robe all the way open and starts kissing his way down my belly, his fingertips flitting down the side of my ribs as I grab his hair and decide he should maybe not shave today.

Because that scratchiness feels wonderful as his face settles between my legs.

"Jesse." It's kind of a half moan, half warning.

He looks up at me, but he continues to lick me. "What?" He whispers it in that husky I'm-about-to-fuck-you voice I love so much.

"We're going to be late."

"It's your jet, Emma. It leaves when we're on it."

"I know, but Miles and Christopher are celebrating the holidays in Vegas this year—"

"I know. I bought them that trip."

"—and they want to get there."

"Their Bellagio reservation isn't until tomorrow. They're spending the night in Key West."

"How do you know they're spending the night in Key West?"

"Because your mom invited them to the street party tonight."

"Oh, my God. My fuckin' mom! She's so in my business! Why can't she just butt out?"

His hands slide up the inside of my legs and then his thumbs are gently pushing the lips open so his tongue can get better access to my sweet spot. He grins. His tongue does this little swirly thing that I love. "I guess I can stop. If you really want me to."

Fuck it. It is my jet. "Well… if you're going to

insist, then keep going, Mr. Bossy."

He chuckles and follows my order. And I forget about everything. I forget about my meddling mother and Jesse's obvious weird mood this morning. I forget about the crew and their trip to Vegas. I forget about everything except this moment right here and the way Jesse's tongue feels as he kisses me, and sucks me, and licks me in all the right places and all the right ways.

He hikes my knees up and can I just say? I love that. God, I love that. I love everything he does. There isn't a single thing about this man I don't adore.

Plus he's talented in the sex department. I feel like a goddess when Jesse Boston is sexing me.

I let his attention wash over me like a warm ray of the Key West sun. I wriggle a little every time his tongue twists and swirls around my throbbing clit and I know it won't take much more for Jesse to build me up and get my release.

But I don't want to come on his face. Not this time. So I grab his hair and pull his head up. With force, but also gently.

"What?" He chuckles as he nuzzles his chin over my wet pussy. "What are you doing?"

"I want to climb in your lap. I want to ease down on your hard cock and let you fill me up. I want to—"

He grabs me before I can finish and a moment

later, we've switched places. I'm squealing as he leans back into the couch cushions and grabs my hips as he innuendoes me with his eyebrows. "Done."

I place my hands on either side of his scratchy cheeks, lean down, and kiss him. Hard. Tasting myself on his lips and his tongue. Then I lift up my hips, reach down, grab his cock, and place it at my entrance.

He grins like a boy as he closes his eyes and lets his head fall to the side a little. And when I sit down on him, he sucks in a breath of air and grips my hips tighter in encouragement.

I love this man. He stole my heart thirteen years ago—no. No, that's not quite right. I gave him my heart thirteen years ago. All he did was accept it.

It's his now. All his and I never want to take it back.

We don't fuck, per se. This isn't fucking. Last night on my office desk? That was fucking. This right here? This is lovemaking. And that's so corny, and silly, and cliché—but I don't care.

This right here—the way we move together, slowly and perfectly, like we are two pieces that fit together in a way that can't be forced or manufactured—this is the dictionary definition of lovemaking.

We kiss as I rock in his lap. And he says things like, "You're beautiful," and "I love you," and "You are the sweetest, most adorable woman I've ever laid eyes on and we were meant to be together. And next spring, when I'm standing at that altar, waiting for you to walk down the aisle to me, I think my heart will explode with gratitude. Because you, Emma Dumas, are my world."

It's a lot of words. Probably more than needs to be said during lovemaking. But they do more for my sexual arousal than his tongue just did a minute ago.

These words of his... they are nourishment.

He is like food, and water, and air to me.

I feel the release building. I feel the excitement of being everything to him as his cock slides up and down inside me. I feel the rising tide of pleasure coming to a peak and then...

Climax.

If I were standing, it would knock me down. I'm sitting in his lap and I suddenly feel like I'm floating. Up, up, up—and then his arms wrap around me and pull me back to him. Anchor me in his embrace as our hearts frantically beat inside our bodies. Together, but separate.

I rest my head on his shoulder and sigh.

"Damn, woman," he says. "Just... *damn*." Then he's grabbing my hair and pulling my mouth to his, and we're kissing like two teenagers on a yacht down in Key West who just figured out they're soulmates.

We stay like that for a little bit, neither of us ready

to break the moment and pull ourselves back into reality.

We are flying to Key West. In a few hours we will be there. There will be a big street party tonight with lots of loud, boisterous laughing and talking. And lots of food. And lots of love.

But right now, this is all the love we need. It takes many more minutes before he slaps the sole of my foot and says, "OK. We can start our holiday now."

I roll off him and settle into the couch with my eyes closed. "I could sleep for days right now. I could sleep right through Christmas." I crack open one eye. "Maybe we should?"

Jesse is leaning back into the couch cushions with his eyes closed too, a broad, charming, satisfied grin on his face. "Should what?"

"Stay home."

He opens both eyes. "What?"

"We could just have a quiet holiday all to ourselves. Never put clothes. No make-up, no suits, no parties. Just nine days of sex."

"That's a joke, right?"

I shrug. "We are grown-ups, right? We can do whatever we want."

"Emma Dumas. Your mother would flip her lid if we didn't show up for Christmas. Remember that weekend in September when we couldn't make it for Saturday night dinner?"

"God, don't remind me." My mother forced the whole family to get in the fucking Suburban and drive up to the city to bring Saturday night dinner to us.

It took twelve hours. Twelve hours of my poor giant brothers and father stuffed into a Suburban with grocery bags and ice chests filled with food—because God knows she couldn't shop for dinner when she got here, right?—and then when they got here they took over my apartment.

Don't get me wrong, it was fun. And sorta amazing. That my mother would go to all that trouble just to have her precious dinner night with her family.

But Jesse is right. She would bring Christmas here. And I can't in good conscience force my poor brothers to endure another twelve-hour drive with groceries and presents jammed between them, not to mention a Christmas tree strapped to the roof of the Suburban, just because we want to have a sex holiday.

"OK." I sigh. "Let's do this."

As much as I complain about my bossy mother, being on the jet and on our way to Key West is exciting.

I don't care how many times I have made this trip in the past, or how many times I'll make it in the future, the moment I see the jet waiting for us on the tarmac the only thing I can think about is that one-up date I took Jesse on last summer and how my family fell in love with him immediately.

Well, maybe not Alonzo. And Tony has fantasy fights in some MMA game he plays with a guy who looks suspiciously like Jesse. But Luke loves him.

That date, though.

I had just spent ten million dollars to buy Jesse in a bachelor auction, drugged him with roofies, kidnapped him with my three best friends, tied him up in our lake house basement, and then hate-fucked him. Sorta. I let him eat me out, then I walked out, flashing him the finger as I squealed my tires.

The whole day was a plan of revenge. Both on his part, and mine. And since he technically was in control that day—holding a fake blood test over my head that proved he'd been drugged the night before—I was fuming when he insisted I had to spend the day with him.

So I came up with the one-up date out of anger, and hate, and schemes of revenge.

How could such a perfect day come out of these emotions?

It still makes my head spin. Also makes me question the sanity of the universe. Like… who was the insane god-thing that decided "Hey, we can totally turn this hate-date into a love connection," once he/she/it got wind of my plan?

But then… then I realize it was me.

I did that, not the universe god-thing. I'm the one who planned the day from top to bottom. And it was perfect. Jesse Boston fell in love with me the moment I started banging my head to *Smells Like Teen Spirit* in that matte-black Lamborghini outside my building. And then he slipped on a rock or something, a patch of mud on the hillside called Emma Dumas Gets Revenge, and the rest is history, baby. Or maybe *her*story?

Ha.

I make my own future. I'm totally in charge of the whole thing.

So I'm smiling big with this realization when Miles comes at me with the jet's satellite phone on a silver tray. I sorta love that Miles takes his jet-butler duties so seriously. He and his partner—our pilot, Christopher—they both totally deserve this holiday trip to Vegas that Jesse bought them.

"What's this?" I ask Miles, pointing to the tray.

"Your mother, Miss Dumas. She just called. Says

it's urgent that she speak to you."

"My God." I sigh, but pick up the phone.

Jesse is waggling his eyebrows at me from across the table as he stuffs mini-rolls into his mouth. I hold up a finger. We had sex like forty-five minutes ago, but hey, if he wants to punch a hole in our mile-high frequent-flyer card, I'm up for another round.

But my mother. I know how she is. She only calls me on the jet when she's manic about something. So I get up and go into the bedroom, sliding the pocket door closed behind me, before I say, "Yes, Mom. What's up?"

"Oh, my stars," she starts. "Do you know who I just bumped into?"

"What? Who? What are we talking about?"

"Your best friend! Can you believe it?"

"You bumped into—*Natalie?*" I choose Natalie over Hannah and Mila because she's the only one I can picture being in Key West this morning without me knowing about it, not because I consider her my number one bestie. They are all equally best in my mind. Nat is a little bit crazy though, and a whole lot spontaneous. So she actually could've been in Key West talking to my mom this morning.

"Natalie? No. *Karen.* You remember Karen, right?"

I should, since my mother is insisting she's my

bestie. But—"No. Mom. Who the hell is Karen?"

"Language, Emma. Why must you use those curse words?"

I sigh and roll my eyes.

"I heard that," my mother says. "And don't roll your eyes at me."

"Mom. I'm thirty thousand feet in the air. On a jet. Flying to you at this very moment. I will literally be in your house in less than three hours. Why are you calling me on a satellite phone about some stranger named Karen?"

"Stranger? Karen, Emma! Karen Krakken! She used to live behind us, and sorta kitty-wonkus diagonally? Remember?"

Oh. My. God. Karen fucking Krakken.

"She's in town! In fact, she bought her old house last month. She and her family—the new family—she has two kids, Chauncey and Chance, and her husband, Chad—not the old family—they're back! Isn't that wonderful? She just moved in last week and came over this morning to say hi! I told her you were coming and that you'd be so excited to see her again! Oh, this is going to be the best Christmas ever. All the old friends back. The street party will be so wonderful with Karen and her family there, don't you think?"

I am… at a loss for words at the moment. Because

Karen fucking Krakken is... well, you know, sometimes people get a last name that totally fits them? Kraken Karen, which is what we all used to call her back in junior high when she did live kitty-wonkus diagonally behind us, she was a fuckin' kraken. I get it, the spelling is slightly off, but trust me. If ever there was a person who ascended out of the depths of the ocean to terrorize and trap you in her sticky tentacles, it's Karen fucking Krakken.

And seriously? Who marries a man called Chad and names their kids Chauncey and Chance? I bet she drives a minivan and is already campaigning to be the PTA president, just like her kraken mother back in the day.

"No."

"Yes!" my mother exclaims. "Yes. It's her! I promise you. She looks the same and everything. You won't believe how great she looks, Emma. I've invited her to our street party tonight. She's bringing a casserole for the family and friends potluck. I think she said mac and cheese flaky-bake. Have you ever heard of that? I'm not sure what it is exactly, but I'm confident I'm going to love it. We loved her and her family so much, remember? She was always..."

I tune my mother out. Because I certainly do remember Karen Krakken. She was a nightmare bully in junior high. And her family was the worst. The worst. Her brother used to spit on me when I was jumping rope. And her little sister used to pee in the backyard. Not *their* backyard. Our backyard. That was before we bought the whole cul-de-sac and put up privacy fences.

But that was nothing compared to the kind of monster treatment I got from Karen. Every time a boy took interest in me she swooped in and stole him. Or even if she didn't steal him, she ruined the connection we were about to make.

Fuckin' Karen.

That internet meme—*Look, Karen…* yeah. That's her. She's *that* Karen.

"Mom," I say, because she's still talking about how much we love, love, love the Krakken family. "She is not invited to the street party. No way. Take it back."

"Take it back? Why?"

Oh, my God. How does my mother not know how much I hate Karen? "We were never best friends. We weren't even frienemies. She cannot come to our street party!"

"Of course she can! It's open to everyone, Emma. And you know, it's bad manners to take back a party invitation. I don't even think that's a thing. Jack? JACK!"

"What?" I hear my father say in Key West.

"It's not a thing, right?"

"Mom. Listen."

"No," my father says, which he's only doing to agree with my bossy mom. He probably doesn't even know what we're talking about.

"See!" She's beaming a smile. I just know it.

"Mom. Listen."

"What time will you get here? You're not going to be late, right? I told Karen the street party starts at three o'clock sharp."

"I'm on the jet, Mom. It's nine AM. There is no possible way I won't be there by three."

But maybe there should be a way? Maybe we should break down in like... Gainesville? And spend a nice time in some two-star hotel's dirty pool? That has to be better than spending an evening with Kraken Karen and her alliteratively-named family, right?

"Great! Then we'll see you soon! I can't wait for you and Karen to reconnect. I told her all about Jesse too. She's swooning over him already!"

"I bet she is. But listen—"

"Byeeeeee!"

The call drops and I just stare at the phone for a moment. Then I open the pocket door and say, "Turn the plane around!"

CHAPTER FIVE

JESSE

Let me explain all the ways that Miles is a very cool dude.

One. When he found me passed-out half-naked on the jet portion of the now infamous one-up date between Emma and I, dude didn't even blink. Just picked up my soiled shirt with a pair of sterling-silver tongs and asked me if I'd like him to have it cleaned. And not only did he do that, it was pressed and inside a little plastic package with a satin bow on the zipper when it was returned to me.

Two. Now that I've had a chance to get to know the guy—we have almost religiously taken the weekend trip down to Key West for Saturday night dinner since last summer—I've learned a lot about him. For instance, he has no family. None. Not a single brother, or mother, or cousin in the entire world. Just his partner, Christopher, our pilot. That's why he digs being Emma's jet butler. And let's face it, for the salary he's making to be on call, he's kinda living the life.

Three. He's like a world-class champion poker player. Like… seven-card stud is his *jam*. And good old Miles here, he can count cards. He told me he's like a Rain Man when it comes to numbers. A savant with social skills, if you will. This is why I offered him an all-expenses-paid trip to Vegas as his Christmas present.

Usually Emma likes to work on the jet ride down to Key West. It makes her feel like she's not ruining the planet with her air travel if she doesn't enjoy it too much—which, OK, I don't buy into myself. But I support her privilege guilt.

So while she works, I chat with Miles. And I learned that fuckin' Miles has been in the World Series Cup of Poker six times. And he was the grand champion twice.

Just for clarification here, this is not the World *Series* of Poker. Nor is it the World *Cup* of Poker. Both of those are legit games. No, my man Miles here? He's into the underground black-ops version of said games. I'm talking secret Illuminati versions of said games.

Which I'm totally intrigued by since the Boston family is all involved in some secret shit ourselves.

At first, I was a little afraid of Miles after he spilled

these beans. I mean, what are the chances that some underground, shadow-poker guy like Miles would end up being my girl's jet butler when said girl is also involved with me? An underground, shadow something-or-other youngest brother in a sorta Mob family?

But… I was paranoid back then. This was right when Joey found out his kid called him and just before Johnny disappeared in the Caribbean to look for Charlotte Kane. I was a little high-strung at the time.

Since then things have calmed down. I'm still not one hundred percent sure what Johnny did to wrangle us all out of the whole money-making ceremony our family has been running for at least two generations, possibly more. But… it's all working out, I guess. Everyone seems pretty chill about it.

And the money still flows. So… I should probably think harder about all this, but now is not the time. All I want to hear about right now is what my man Miles will be up to in Vegas over Christmas.

"It's a five-million-dollar pot," Miles is telling me. We're chillaxing at the table and scarfing down some Barbie and Ken mini rolls while Emma takes her mom-call in the bedroom.

"Five large, huh? Damn, dude. And you won this twice? Why do you even work?"

Miles does have that trademark butler smugness to him, but he wears it better than most butlers. It doesn't come off as pretentious. More like… wise. Yeah. Wise. I really dig Miles and his confident body of knowledge.

"I know it sounds counterintuitive, but"—I also like all the big words Miles uses. I always feel smart when we talk because even though I'm not into using big words, I have a fairly nice vocab myself—"I don't like risk, sir."

"No? So… how the hell did you get into poker anyway? Because yeah." I point at him. "That *is* counterintuitive."

"I was a homeless kid living on the streets of Pittsburgh—"

"No shit!"

"—and I got hired by a man called Shoes to help him cheat during the local Mob pinochle game at Freddy's Pizza in Bethel Park."

"Whoa. Dude."

"Yes," Miles says. "It was one of my weaker moments in life. But Shoes was an astute player. And quite reasonable. He didn't *need* to cheat, pinochle was his"—and Miles points to me for this part—"*jam*, sir." I just chuckle. "But everyone loses eventually. He hired me when he heard about my math skills and he taught me how to count cards."

"But didn't they know?"

"Of course they knew, sir. But Shoes was, as they say, big time. And his uncle ran the pizza place. So as long as he didn't cheat too often, they let it go. But everyone's goodwill runs out eventually. He cheated the wrong guy, they killed him, took me to Chicago, and put me to work as the little footman for the head Mob boss there."

"Interesting," I say, nodding my head. "So that's how you became a butler and a poker player."

"Exactly, sir."

"So… how did you get out of the Mob? If you don't mind me asking."

"The boss I was working for was killed by his son and I was thrown out of the house. I was in my twenties by then and playing lots of cards on the side. I had been to every underground tournament the old boss played in for years. So I simply started going to the secret games myself. Everything worked out from there. But then I saw Miss Dumas' ad on the *Modern Butler* website and applied, thinking this would be a good way to work full-time and pay taxes."

"Yeah." I'm nodding and pointing at him. "They always get the bad guys with tax evasion, don't they?"

"They always do, sir. You can still be part of the secret shady underground these days. But you must have an up-and-up side to you as well. It's all trackable now."

"Good thinking, Miles."

"Thank you, sir."

And that's when Emma throws open the jet bedroom pocket door and says, "Turn the plane around!"

Miles and I both get to our feet. "Whoa, there, bossy babe. What's going on? Is everything OK?"

"No," she squeals. "Everything is not OK! Do you know what my mother just did?"

Miles and I both make those all-teeth smiles, preparing ourselves for Emma's explanation. Because let's face it, we all know how bossy her mother is. She even bosses Miles. And if I'm being completely honest here, when Miles is in the room, dude's the boss. He just has this all-knowing, all-powerful boss vibe, ya know?

But bossy Silvia can even overpower my brother Johnny, so Miles doesn't have a chance when Silvia gets her bossy on.

"She invited Kraken Karen to our street party tonight!"

"No," Miles says.

So I say, "She did not," even though I have no clue what the hell that sentence means. Kraken Karen? Did

I hear that right? I'm not sure.

"See!" Emma is pointing at Miles. "Even you get it." Then she pauses. "Wait. How do you know Kraken Karen?"

Miles presses his lips together and bows his head a little. And I'm like one hundred percent sure this is the moment that Miles has no clue. I'm about to write the date down for posterity because it's got to be a one-time thing.

But surprise, surprise, Miles does know Kraken Karen. Because he says, "I'm very familiar with the Krakken family, ma'am. They are, quite literally, the kraken incarnate."

"See!" Emma says again, turning to me. "Everyone knows the Krakkens are krakens!"

"OK, hold on, babe. Slow down a sec. Because I'm not in the know here. Who the hell is Kraken Karen?"

"Some pretentious bully bitch from my past, that's who! Her little sister used to pee in our backyard and her brother used to spit on me when I was jumping rope. Aaaaand…" She nods her head and drags that word out like this is the real point she's trying to make. "If she thinks she's gonna wrap her filthy tentacles around your scrumptious muscly arms, she's got another think coming!"

I look down at my muscly arms, taking a moment

to appreciate the fact that Emma finds them to be scrumptious.

"Ma'am." Miles is taking over now. "Is this request to turn the plane around a legitimate one? Or just a manic response to the news?"

See? God. This dude is so... *on* it.

But I can tell that Emma is about to say, "Legitimate," so I have to intervene. "Emma. Let's think about this." Because there's no way we're not landing in Key West. Her mother would hunt us down and boss our asses back to Florida so fast, our heads would be on backwards from all the spinning when we arrived. "It's Christmas Eve eve, babe. Your whole family expects us to show up for festivities. Are you really gonna let some sea monster called Karen ruin our holiday?"

She considers this. "Yes."

I laugh and cross the distance between us to pull her into a tight hug. "Come on. You can handle Kraken Karen, right? It's just one party. A few hours and it's over. You'll never have to see her again."

"No. You don't understand, Jesse. Kraken Karen moved back in." She grabs her hair with both hands. "Oh, my God. She now lives behind us! Like directly behind us! We will literally be able to look out our bedroom window and see her stupid face across our backyards. Before it was just kitty-wonkus diagonal and now it's just... behind us!"

Even Miles is confused at this string of words.

"What?" I say.

"Her old house is the house right behind the Emma and Jesse cottage on Dumas Street! Jesus Christ. I can't do it. I won't do it."

"Emma, come on. How bad can she be?"

"You have no idea. I have stories."

I glance at Miles, who just shrugs. "The Krakkens are terrible."

"Terrible... I'm-gonna-kill-you Mob-boss style? Or just your everyday, ordinary terrible?" Emma shoots me a look. "Well, I just need to make sure. If Miles knows the Krakkens they could be—" But Miles is making a motion of zip-your-lip-Jesse, so I stop. "What?"

"She's just horrible, Jesse," Emma continues. "Just... horrible. And the minute she sees you, she's gonna latch onto you with those hooked-tentacle claws of hers and—"

"OK, stop." I hold up a hand. "Really? Come on, Emma. You're my girl. You're my jam, baby! There isn't a kraken alive that could change my mind about you."

She pouts. And oh, my God. That pout. I mean,

Emma pouts all the time. It's a perpetual pout. That's just her sexy lips in their natural glory. And can I just say, she's got the sexiest fucking lips I've ever seen. Mad, sad, angry, happy—that pout does me in.

I hug her tighter and then kiss her softly. "Relax, babe. Seriously. It's gonna be fine. One party. That's it. One party and we're done with Kraken Karen. We'll close the drapes in the bedroom and never look out the window again. Hell, we can stay in another cottage if you want. Some of them are empty, right?"

"I don't know for sure." She sniffs. It's a fake, pouty sniff, but that's OK. She's allowed to fake-cry if she wants. "We're usually all booked up for the holidays. But I guess we could stay in Zach's cabin."

"See!" I nod at Miles. "It's all settled. That's perfect. I'm sure Zach would love for us to stay with him. Little fucker owes me, anyway. I let him stay with me for thirteen years."

And it does seem settled. Emma calms down, eats a couple dozen Barbie and Ken rolls, drinks three or seventeen glasses of champagne orange fizzy, and half-listens in tipsy fascination as Miles whips out a map of Vegas that details the route and check-in process for his secret underground black-ops poker game tomorrow night.

And just a little while after that's all done, we're getting ready to land. Miles is cleaning up, and Emma is calm again, resting in her super-luxurious leather seat with her eyes closed, Kraken Karen forgotten.

And then we're on the ground. And the winter sun is beaming down on me like a big ol' welcome-home bath of UV light.

I love it.

I love this place.

I could live here.

If I could talk Emma into moving the Bright Berry Beach corporate offices down here, I would. But there's no way she'd come back to Key West for good. She's a city girl now.

And even though I spent almost my whole life without Joey and Johnny, it's really been great having them around again. Makes me feel like we're kids again.

Then we're in the car heading towards Dumas Street, which, to my surprise, has been blocked off with orange cones. "What's this?" I ask Emma when the town car pulls over to the side of the road.

"The party."

"You block off the cul-de-sac? And... is that a shaved ice stand I see in the middle of the street?"

"Every year, Mr. Boston. And yes, that's shaved ice. I'm gonna buy you a cherry vanilla in a Dumas souvenir cup the minute it opens. The Dumas street party is a very big deal on the island. Even the tourists come to celebrate the palm-tree lighting."

I grin. Positively smirk as I picture our shared shaved-ice past. "God, I love this place."

The driver grabs our luggage and we start rolling our wheelie suitcases down the uneven sidewalk towards Zach's cottage. I thought for sure Emma would forget about Kraken Karen and that staying with Zach was just a heat-of-the-moment overreaction, but nope. My bossy girl is on it. We lug all the suitcases up the front porch steps of Zach's cottage and bang on the screen door.

He opens it shirtless and a little out of breath. "Uh… Jesse!" His confusion turns to a smile and he rallies, opening the door to bring it in for a hug. "Dude! Merry Christmas!" Then he looks around, spots our luggage, and once again becomes confused. "What's up?"

"We're staying with you," Emma says.

"You… are?"

"Yeah," I say. "Fucking Kraken Karen is back and our house overlooks her backyard or some shit. So… you don't mind, right?" But that's when I notice a naked girl walking into the kitchen behind him. "Oh." I glance over my shoulder at Emma.

She's wincing. "You have… a guest."

Zach looks over his shoulder too, then slips outside and closes the main door behind him. "Yeah. You guys, I didn't know. I invited this girl to hang with us."

"Us?" Emma and I both say at the same time.

"Luke, me, her…" Zach grins.

"Ohhhhhhh," I say.

"Oh, oh, oh," Emma echoes. "Gotcha." She looks at me. "OK. Well, that was TMI for me. Let's go. I'm sure one of the cottages is empty."

"No, they're full," Zach says, then shrugs. "Holidays."

"Well… obviously Luke's cottage isn't *occupied*, right? We can just stay there."

"Actually…"

"Actually *what*?" Emma is about to lose it.

"He lives here now. We… we all live here now. So his cottage is rented too."

Emma sucks in a big breath.

I take over and clap Zach on the shoulder. "It's cool. I got this." Then I open the door, push him back inside, and take Emma's hand. "It's gonna be fine. I promise. Karen who, right? We don't even have to see her. We'll never look out that window again. I'm sure it will be super easy to avoid Kraken—"

"Yooooo-hoooooo! Neighbor girl!"

Emma's whole body goes stiff and she grips both my scrumptious muscly arms so hard, I think her fingernails are leaving marks. "No," she whispers.

"Yooooo-hooooo! Emma! It's me, Karen! Oh, my God! You're heeeeereeee! Yay! Your mom told me—"

"*No*," Emma insists again.

But… Oh, yeah. Kraken Karen is walking up Zach, Luke, and naked girl's front-porch steps beaming her sea-monster smile at me. "You must be Jesse Boston. I've heard a lot about you, mister, but"—she's purring out her words—"none of the descriptions did you justice."

And then I swear to God, she grips my scrumptious, muscly arm right above where Emma is already making her claim and leans in to kiss me on the cheek.

CHAPTER SIX

"What the fuck, Karen? What the hell do you think you're doing? Who comes up to a complete stranger and... and... and acts like a goddamned sex siren right in front of his fucking fiancée?"

Kraken Karen has the nerve to look shocked at my outburst. I'm talking mouth in the shape of an o, and hand over heart, and the whole chin-jutting-backward thing. But my mom was right. She looks exactly the same. Short, blonde, bobby haircut. Pursed lips. And low-cut shirt to show off her goods. And for a moment I'm distracted by that instead of the fact that she just kissed my man and I freaked out about it.

"Oh. Emma. I'm so sorry. I was just excited to see you again. And with this"—she ogles Jesse—"American treasure. The one and only Jesse Boston. Well *done*, Emma. Well done."

I glance at Jesse and find him beaming back at her. What the fuck?

"Excuse me. Eyes over here, buddy." I do the little finger point thing. Him, me, him.

Which only makes Jesse chuckle as he wraps his arms around mine and pulls me into his chest. And for a moment I soften. I go a little squishy at his possessive embrace.

But then… is this just his preemptive move to make sure I don't haul off and hit Kraken Karen in the eye?

"Um… sooo?" We all turn to look at Zach Boston on the other side of the screen door. "Are we good here?" He does one of those backward nods of his head to indicate something behind him. "I've gotta… you know. Finish up in here and then get out there to help Luke with the party tonight."

Jesse waves him off. "Yeah, go. See ya in a few, Zach."

And with that Zach Boston excuses himself from this now very awkward situation on his porch, so now it's just the three of us.

Me. My gorgeous man. And my worst enemy.

I decide the best offense right now is a retreat. "Well, Karen. It was… whatever. We have to go."

I squirm out of Jesse's embrace and grab the handle

of my wheelie suitcase and start dragging it down the porch steps as the driver scrambles with the rest. I point to the house kitty-wonkus diagonally across the street and say, "That's where we're heading, I guess," then look over my shoulder to make sure Kraken Karen isn't trying to hump Jesse's leg while I'm not looking.

She's not. But she's still smiling at him like she wants to.

Jesse dutifully follows me, dragging his own wheelie suitcase down the porch steps, and we don't look back until we're across the street and on the porch of the Emma and Jesse cottage.

Karen is gone.

But instead of being relieved I feel like she's stalking me from the bushes.

Jesse opens the cottage door and waves me in. "Just… forget about her. We're not gonna see her again. We're just gonna close up the curtains and pretend we're the only people in the world."

"Right." But I know it's not true. Kraken Karen is back for a reason. She saw us in the news or something. Our engagement was in the tabloids. They even featured us on some gossipy cable entertainment show the week after Halloween. In fact, according to my mother, that's right around the time she bought her old house.

Something is definitely up with the Kraken.

The driver helps us with our luggage, Jesse tips him, and then he closes the door and turns to face me with a sigh. "Come on, Emma. It's Christmas. We're here with your family, there's a huge party tonight and a big Christmas Eve dinner tomorrow. Then the big day, and lots of pie, and mashed potatoes. And then it's a whole week of exploring beaches, and diving, and having sex on secret sandbars."

I smile, picturing it. He's right. Karen won't be around for any of that stuff. So what if she manages to squirm her way into our tree-trimming street party? She won't get any closer than that. For sure. It's just family after tonight.

But… God. I just can't shake it. "She's like a bad omen," I tell Jesse.

"No, she's not. It's just… she's just a minor blip. That's all. She's got no staying power. And besides, we don't really live here. We live three and half hours away by private jet. She can't follow us back to the city."

"I know. But… I just don't understand why she's back. She's been gone for like fifteen years. And then all of a sudden we're engaged, and in the news, and she's here. Why?"

"Maybe she missed you?"

I cough out a laugh. "No. That's not it. She was my worst enemy."

Jesse makes a face at me. "Then why does your mother like her so much?"

I tsk my tongue. "I never told her about all the things Karen did back when we were kids."

"Maybe you should tell her now?"

"What's the point?"

"Well… your mom would take your side. You have to know that. Your family is fiercely overprotective. One word to Alonzo about—"

"Oh, no. You don't understand. He *dated* her!"

"What?"

"Yeah. For almost a year when he was a senior in high school. And she is the one who broke it off with him! He was crushed."

"Wow. OK. Well… I didn't see that coming."

"I know. But she's not back for Alonzo, because she's married."

"That logic holds true for me too, Emma. I'm taken."

"It's different." I chew my lip, trying to work it out. "Something is fishy here."

"Well… I don't know. I think you're making too big of a deal about this. Just…" He wraps his arms around my middle and leans his forehead against mine.

Which makes me smile and only think about him. Because yeah. *Well done, Emma Dumas. Well done.* Jesse Boston is the catch of the century.

So... is this just my own insecurities showing?

Maybe.

I drape my arms around his neck. "You're right. I'm gonna just... let it go. It's Christmas, we're here with our family, and we're gonna have a great time."

He kisses me and all my dark, evil thoughts about Karen fade away in an instant. And when he breaks away and presses his forehead against mine, he says, "Ya know, she could be after you and not me."

Which makes me giggle. "Right."

"You're hot," he says. "You're bossy. You're super-rich, and super-smart, and super-pretty too. In fact, now I'm a little worried she might steal you away from me."

"Stop it. You're being silly." But I get it. I'm being silly too.

"So... are we ready then? Should we go find your mom and dad? Get this street party started?"

I kiss him one more time, lingering in it just a little bit longer than I normally would, then whisper, "Yeah. I'm ready. Let's go make a ruckus."

The rest of the afternoon is filled with last-minute details. Jesse joins the volunteers with getting all the lights and ornaments on the big palm tree in my parents' front yard ready for the lighting ceremony and I make sure all the vendors set up in the middle of the street have what they need.

Dumas Street is the length of five cottages on either side, plus one—my parents' place and family home—at the top of the cul-de-sac, right in the middle.

The Emma and Jesse cottage is on my parents' immediate right as you're looking at the house, and across the street from us is Alonzo's cottage. Next to us is Tony's place, and across from Tony's place is Luke's, which is now filled with some random holiday family because Luke is living a sexy dream life with Zach and naked girl right next door. The rest of them are all rentals.

The street isn't very wide, and almost all of it is taken up with street vendors and food trucks, which are lined up down the middle. Yes, there's shaved ice. There's always a shaved ice truck. But we've got a beer garden, and a pizza truck, and even a pop-up Cuban restaurant. Not to mention a merry-go-round and a Ferris wheel at the bottom of the street and even some carnival games.

It's a pretty big deal to rent one of the Dumas

cottages during the annual tree-lighting ceremony. And while this is not really a city event, the whole island gets in on it. It's just a big ol' night of fun.

Back when I was a kid it was a block party. This was before my parents bought up the cottages and they were filled with neighbors. We had a potluck, and that tradition continues today, but it's only for family and volunteers now. It happens in the back yard after the palm tree is lit up and the festivities are winding down. And all the kids back when I was little would play in the blocked-off street. Some years we had fireworks. That was the big deal back when this all started.

I can honestly say I never imagined it would turn into this.

Later, Jesse and I walk next door to my parents' house and immediately get a warm, over-the-top welcome from my mother—who wants to feed us everything in the kitchen—and suffocating bear hugs from my father. Alonzo punches Jesse on the arm way too hard, but Jesse laughs it off like a good sport, and then Tony does his famous hug swing when he shows up.

I watch Jesse as all this goes down.

My family is… big. Not big as in a lot of people, though four kids and parents is larger than most families these days. But big as in boisterous. We are loud, and we talk over people, and we are all very, very bossy.

But Jesse seems to love it. And I love that he loves it. He soaks it up. Takes all the hits my brothers throw at him in stride. And when we're down here he never seems to stop smiling.

And my family loves him. Alonzo gives him a hard time, but I can tell Jesse is growing on him. Alonzo invited us to go deep-sea fishing with him this week. That's no small invitation when it comes to Alonzo. He takes his swordfish seriously.

So I forget all about Karen. I see her and her family every now and then throughout the afternoon and evening. But she keeps her distance and that's the best I can hope for, I guess.

It's about eight in the evening when I break away from my job as vendor liaison and find Jesse standing in the shaved ice line.

"What are you getting?" I ask, sliding up next to him and slipping my hand in his.

"Cherry vanilla in a souvenir cup." He winks. "Wanna share with me?"

"You bet."

He orders. The girl—a teenager, just like I was that first afternoon when Jesse and I first met on this very island, just a few blocks away—smiles at Jesse like he's the best thing to happen to her in her whole life.

I know the feeling, chickie. Trust me. I know the feeling.

She turns to us, handing the pink cup over, but then stops and gets a weird look on her face.

"Everything OK?" Jesse asks.

"Um… uh…" the girl stammers. And then she turns the cup around and points to the picture on the front.

It says 'Dumas Street Tree Lighting' and there's a picture of me and my whole family on the front. Only this year Jesse's face is on the cup too.

Jesse laughs. "Will you look at that?" Jesse says, taking the cup. "I'm family."

"You're family," I agree.

We take the shaved ice and walk back over to our cottage and share it as we sit on the top step of the porch and watch the people all around us.

We sit in silence for a while.

Not that anything around us is silent. It's nothing but noise, actually. But it's the peaceful kind of noise. The bustle of happy people. The shouts of excited teenagers at the top of the Ferris wheel and the squeals of sugared-up kids as they chase each other in the grass of the cottage front yards.

"I can't believe this is your life," Jesse suddenly says.

"What? What do you mean?"

"It's all just so…"

"Over the top?"

"No." He shakes his head. "But… yeah. In the best way though. It's so… different than how I grew up."

Which gets me curious. Jesse hasn't talked about his childhood much. Not since that first night we reconnected and ate ice cream at the Tastee-Freez after the bachelor auction. "How did you spend Christmas Eve eve?"

He inhales deeply and holds his breath for a moment, then lets it out slowly. "We didn't."

"Oh. Well, that's understandable. Most families don't have a tradition like this."

"I mean, we didn't celebrate Christmas at all after I was like… ten, I guess."

I frown. I do remember him saying something like that before. "But when you took me down to the family floor in the Bossy, you pointed out where the tree was."

"In front of the windows."

"Yeah. So you must have some good memories from that time, right?"

He sighs, looking out at all the people in the street for a moment. Then he looks at me. "No, Emma. I don't. I mean, there were a few years when we got presents and had a tree. The only real tradition that I even remember from that time is the stockings we had over the fireplace. And that's only because Johnny wrote our names on them in red glitter glue. But most years? It was just another day."

Now I frown. "Oh. I don't think I realized that."

"But…" He smiles at me and takes my hand. His is cold from holding the shaved ice cup. "There were a few years when Johnny tried. Once he chopped down a little evergreen shrub out in the Bossy courtyard and hauled it upstairs."

"What?"

"I swear to God. He chopped down what was basically a bush, hauled it upstairs, and then we went on this massive hunt for Christmas shit so we could decorate it."

"How old were you?"

"Mmm… maybe six?"

"So he was eight?"

"Yeah. Eight."

"Did you find the Christmas boxes?"

"No. And I was pretty sad about that because I looked really hard for those glitter-glue stockings. But we did find Easter stuff. And we decorated the tree with pink and green Easter grass and filled up the baskets with forgotten junk-treasure we found while we were searching for the Christmas shit, and those were our presents that year."

And even though this is kinda sad, it's also kinda cool too. These three brothers found a way to celebrate. "Was it fun?"

"I guess. Sure. I guess it was, even though it wasn't really a Christmas."

"What was in your Christmas basket?"

"Oh, man. This kinda was fun. Johnny and Joey were good junk-treasure hunters. I got an old World War II medal, a glow-in-the-dark yo-yo, and a whole bunch of metal toy soldiers that I'm pretty sure were part of some very expensive custom chess set."

"What did you give them? Do you remember?"

"I remember." He's smiling big now. "I found this little dog statue for Johnny. He always did want a dog, even when we were kids. It was kinda ugly. And it was actually probably an ashtray."

I laugh.

"But he loved it. I wonder where that thing went?" He ponders this for a moment. "I dunno. But he had it around for a long time. Maybe it's still up there? Up in his apartment?"

"You should go look."

"I don't think that place is ours anymore. And besides, Johnny probably wouldn't like me nosing around in his shit."

"And what did you get Joey?"

"Joey... I found Joey this cool sword. It was a real one too."

"What kind of sword?"

"You know, like one of those martial arts swords. A katana or something. He always wanted to be a ninja growing up." Jesse snaps his fingers. "You know what holiday we did do, though?"

"Which?"

"Halloween. Joey was always a ninja. Every freaking year. We would dress up and go trick-or-treating inside the building."

"What?"

"Yeah." He laughs. "Thinking about it now, I'm kinda embarrassed. Like... what were all those people thinking about us? Not all the floors were ours, ya know? They're actual companies. Big-time companies. And here come the Boston brothers begging for candy. They must've wondered, *Who the fuck is taking care of these kids? Don't they have parents?*"

"But they couldn't say anything, could they?"

"Nah. We owned the building. And my father was

a scary dude. They gave us lots of shit. Filled up our pillow cases with candy. Or if they didn't have candy—because no trick-or-treaters were supposed to be showing up at the end of a freaking workday, right?"

"Right."

"So sometimes we got office supplies instead. We had a lot of staplers at our house."

I lean into him, feeling simultaneously happy and sad at his childhood memories. "Still," I say, after a few moment of quiet introspection. "It's special in its own way, don't you think?"

"My childhood? Yeah. Definitely not typical."

"It was Johnny," I say.

"What?"

"Taking care of you kids. It was Johnny."

"Yeah. It was always Johnny."

"What's he doing for Christmas?"

"Nothing, I guess. I asked him last night at the party and he said, 'I don't do church.'"

"He doesn't have to do church," I say, giggling.

"I told him that. He didn't seem to get it."

"So they're doing nothing? No tree? No presents? And Megan is… pregnant?"

"Yeah."

"Why didn't we invite them to come down here with us? What is Joey doing? Surely they're getting a tree? For Maisy, at least."

"Maisy is spending Christmas at the Kane estate. Joey didn't think it was fair to take her away from her little sister for the holiday. So he's taking her for New Year's and having Christmas then."

"Call them."

"What?"

"Right now. Call them and tell them to come down here."

Jesse points to the street filled with people. "There's not even an empty cottage, Emma. Where would they stay?"

"Who cares? My parents have two spare bedrooms. Some of them can stay in our old bedrooms. Or we can make Alonzo and Tony stay with the parents and Joey and Johnny can take their cottages."

"I'm sure Alonzo would love that idea."

"I could make him. He'd do it for me."

"Nah. I mean… I would like to have them here. But it would be a huge inconvenience."

"Oh, we're calling them," I say, reaching into his pants pocket for his phone. "Right now. At least extend an invitation. And if they say no, then fine. But maybe they feel left out? That would be terrible. Oh, my God. When I tell my mother about this oversight, she's going to go ballistic. She will insist. She will fly up there herself and drag them all back here. Please. Call them."

"Emma. It's too late."

"It's not. I promise."

"At least ask your family first. If they say it's OK, then I'll call and extend the invitation. But don't get your hopes up. My brothers aren't into family shit like this."

"Done. Let's go ask her right now. They're getting ready to light the tree anyway." I stand up, and take his hand, tugging on it to make him get to his feet.

He does. But he pulls me towards him, staring into my eyes for a moment. Then he leans down and kisses me, whispering, "You're the best present ever, Emma Dumas. All of you."

And he tastes like a cool slice of cherry-vanilla shaved ice.

CHAPTER SEVEN

I tug Emma down the street towards the giant palm tree in her parents' front yard, trying to see if she will forget about calling up my brothers and inviting them down here. But she doesn't.

"Here." She's shoving the phone at me. "Call them, right now. I'll go let my mom know."

"No. You ask everyone if it will be OK first. Then I'll call."

She stops, forcing me to stop with her, because I've still got a hold of her hand. "Hold on. Do you not want them here?"

"I do. If they want to come."

"Why wouldn't they want to come?"

"It's just…"

So here's what it is. Christmas—and all the holidays, actually, even our birthdays—it's a sore spot

101

for us. Because we tried to get my father interested in celebrating stuff like this when we were younger, and it was always a no. Finally, we just gave up. And I could see it in Johnny's eyes last night when I brought it up. He didn't want to think about it. It's for church, he said. But he knows damn well Christmas is for anyone who wants to participate. Not just people who believe the religious aspects. It's a tradition, and traditions are whatever you want them to be.

But see... we did make Christmas our own. We decided, as a family, a very long time ago, we didn't celebrate this holiday. I don't even know what the original reason was, but it doesn't matter. Trying to invite all my brothers down here for Thanksgiving involved a very circular and frankly tiresome conversation that I don't want to repeat.

If they don't want us all to be together on the holidays, that's their decision.

"I'm gonna go ask right now. And you'll see. Everyone will be thrilled." Emma lets go of my hand and starts powerwalking over to her mother and father, who are standing in front of the giant palm tree, ready to light it up.

The Thanksgiving convo went like this:

Hey, brothers! Now that we're all reconnected through this bizarre secret-society bullshit, would you like to spend

Thanksgiving with my new replacement family in Key West?

Which, OK, probably not the best way to start a conversation about reconnecting our familial ties, but what can I say? I'm a charmer.

They were not impressed, nor were they swayed into participating.

I came to terms with the idea a long time ago that while I do have two brothers, I don't really have a family. I'm OK with that. Emma has enough family energy to make up for what I missed out on. And also, honestly, I don't need all my old family baggage following me into this new life.

I'm walking over to Emma to tell her to forget it when I bump right into Miles. "Hey, dude," I say, tapping him on the shoulder. "What are you doing here? I thought you guys were headed to Vegas?"

Miles smiles at me. And wow, this guy looks totally different when he's not wearing his jet-butler outfit. Right now he's wearing faded jeans and a white t-shirt. And for like three whole seconds I think, *This is Miles, right? Did I just approach a total stranger and act like we're friends?*

But no, Miles smiles. "Master Jesse. Nice to see you in a more personal atmosphere. Christopher and I are heading out later tonight and we'll be ready for Sin City by morning."

I point at him. "Can't miss out on this good time, right?"

"Exactly, sir." He leans in towards me. "But if I may ask…"

"Ask away."

"What is Miss Emma up to?"

We both swing our gazes over to Emma, who is chatting with her mom near the tree as her father talks into a microphone, counting down from ten as he holds the switch to turn on the palm tree lights.

"Don't ask, dude. It's a whole fiasco that involves Joey and Johnny Boston."

"Understood, sir," Miles says. Just as Emma breaks away and starts heading back towards us, her father gets to one, the tree lights up, and the whole street erupts in a loud cheer.

"Hey, Miles!" Emma shouts over the cheers. Then to me, "Come on. I told you she'd say yes!"

"But Alonzo—"

She's already tugging me over to the tree. "Forget Alonzo. He's not in charge of anything. When my mother makes a decision, it's a done deal." She stops in front of the tree and positions me in between Tony and Zach. Zach and I do a little head-nod greeting. Then cameras start flashing and I realize we're in the middle of a photoshoot.

Probably gonna be in the paper tomorrow.

Can't outrun the fucking news. No matter how hard I try.

Emma is talking the whole time. "Call them right now. In my mother's mind, they should be here already. Tell them…"

She goes on and on about what I should tell them. And I can see that there's no way out of this now, so I press Joey's contact first. He doesn't pick up. I'm just in the middle of leaving a message about this new twist when who comes walking up to Emma but Kraken Karen?

I end the call and try to intervene before Emma notices, but too late. Karen is tapping Emma on the shoulder, and shoving a newspaper at her, and her face is nothing but a wide smile.

But it's not really Karen's face I'm watching. It's Emma's.

Because her face is not smiling. Her face has an expression of utter horror as she takes the paper from Karen and then just stares at it in abject panic.

"What?" Emma yells it so loud I can hear it over the excited crowd. "*What?*" Then she whirls to glare at her mother.

"Ut-oh," Miles says, coming up next to me.

"Ut-oh is right. I gotta go." I rush over and take

Emma's hand as she starts saying things like, "What the hell, Mom? What the fuck?"

Silvia is saying, "Language, Emma! There are children here!"

But Emma is giving out no fucks. Or she is. Because 'fuck' is coming out of her mouth at regular intervals.

I tug on her, trying to get her away from, if not her mother and Karen, at least the damn photographers—because they are eating this drama up like starving coyotes—but Emma is putting up a fight. "Why would you do that? Mom! Like... what is going through that brain of yours?"

Silvia is saying, "I just want you to have the perfect wedding, Emma! You're my only daughter. And there's no chance of your brothers ever having a wedding the way they date!"

This makes Luke go, "What's that supposed to mean?"

But I'm pretty sure we all know what that means. I do, at least. Because Joey is in the same kind of relationship and how do you marry two or more people at the same time, right?

Tony says, "God, why do you care if we get married?"

Alonzo is pointing to his father, saying, "You

didn't tell her? What the fuck, Dad? We talked about this."

Which only makes me more confused. But the reporters are swarming now. So I make an executive decision based on many past experiences in the tabloid spotlight and drag Emma through the crowd, not stopping until we're in the side yard of our cottage and then only to open the gate that leads to the backyard.

The whole time she's yelling, "Let go of me! My mother has gone too far this time! The wedding is off!"

"Fuck that," I say, pulling her through the gate and slamming it closed behind us. "I don't care what your mother did. The damn wedding is *not* off!"

Which makes her plant her hands on her hips and huff, "She has ruined everything," as she stomps her foot.

"OK," I say, putting up my hands. "Calm down. Tell me what the hell just happened."

"She told Kraken Karen she can plan my wedding, Jesse! She's some hotshot wedding planner! And"— she stops to suck in a deep breath—"aaaaaand! *My maid of honor*!"

"What?" I laugh. I can't help it.

"It's not funny!"

"Why would she do that?"

"Because apparently, my mother's delusional mind

thinks we're best friends. And Karen just came over to me to say thank you for the invite and she really appreciates my business! I have to pay her! Pay her, Jesse! And she's so excited about the announcement that went out in the paper today! *Today*, Jesse! She had it announced today!"

"So we can like… unannounce it, right? She's not gonna plan our wedding. We didn't sign any contract with her. And she can't be your maid of honor. Mila, or Natalie, or Hannah already has that spot, right?"

"Right! Those girls are my best friends. Not stupid Kraken Karen! But that's not even the worst part. My mother already had her start planning the whole thing. Look!" She thrusts the paper she's still holding at me.

And sure enough, there is a very succinct headline that explains the entire débâcle.

Local Girl to Wed Baby Boston in a Special Dumas Street Event May twenty-fifth.

"Damn." Then I squint my eyes. "Did we set…"

"No! *No*! We did not set a date yet! And we are not getting married in some street festival! But my mother has made all the arrangements! Look at the subheading!"

I don't want to. I really don't. And I'm just about to toss the paper so I don't have to when Emma begins reading it aloud. "'Exclusive pictures of the custom

Vera Wang dress, interview with bridesmaid and wedding planner Karen Krakken Channing, and an inside look at the menu!'"

I have to cover my mouth so I don't laugh.

"It's not funny! It's *my* wedding!"

"I'm not laughing about that, Ems. It's just... Chauncey Channing? What the fuck?"

She looks at me for a moment, so angry. And then her rage breaks and she laughs too. "I know, right? Like who the fuck names their kids Chance and Chauncey Channing?"

I reach for her, pull her in close, and hug her tight. "I get it, Emma. It's your wedding. And it's your day. And you should have everything you want, just the way you want it. And you will. Don't worry. You will."

"I won't!" She pulls back a little. "She's ruined it all!"

"So? We can just... undo it. What kind of dress do you want?"

"I don't know yet! It's a big decision. I need time to just think, ya know? But *I* want to be the one to choose the dress. And I want *us* to be the ones to taste the wedding cake. And I want *us* to have the damn ceremony wherever we want! Maybe we want to get married in the city? Did she ever think of that? Maybe we want to get married in the Bossy, for fuck's sake!

You should have some say in this, right?"

"The Bossy? You're just ranting now, right?"

"Yes. I'm ranting. But would it be so bad if we got married somewhere that's important to you?"

"That place… it's not important, Emma."

"God, you're as delusional as my mother. Of course it's important! You grew up there! It's your home!"

"It's not a home. It's an office building."

She points her finger at me. "Ya know, for a guy who told his badass brother just last night that Christmas isn't about church, just twenty-four hours later you can't grasp the irony of you telling me that a home can't be an office building."

"OK." I sigh. "Let's take a deep breath and just… calm down."

"Calm down!"

But then the gate opens and Emma whirls, ready to throw down if the interloper happens to be Karen Krakken Channing.

I chuckle again. Because my God, that name.

But it's not Karen. It's just Miles.

"Is everything all right, ma'am?"

"Oh, Miles. I'm so sorry you had to see all that. Yes, I'm fine. Or I will be once we cancel the wedding and make another announcement in the paper that the whole thing is off."

Miles shoots me a look of *What the hell is she talking about?*

"Forget it," I tell Miles. "She's just upset because Silvia asked Kraken Karen to plan the wedding and be her bridesmaid."

"Ah," Miles says, understanding. "Well..." Then he laughs. "You could always just elope to Vegas with us tonight and do it your way."

Miles and I have a good laugh about that. 'Yeah. That's a great idea, Miles. We'll just elope tonight and get married in Vegas!"

But Emma is not laughing.

"He's kidding, babe. And so am I."

"I was joking, ma'am. I apologize. This is no time for jokes."

Still, Emma is silent.

"Emma?" I ask.

She brightens. Then she turns to Miles. "Oh, my God. You're a genius, Miles."

"I do my best, ma'am."

Then Emma turns to me. "This really is a great idea! We're eloping to Vegas. Tonight."

"What?"

"You heard me. Fuck it. My mother wants to hire a wedding planner behind my back? Fine. She can have that wedding on May twenty-fifth. Our real wedding is happening tomorrow. December twenty-fourth."

"But…" I look at Miles. "Don't you need like… a venue?"

"Not in Vegas, sir. You just go pull up to the drive-through."

"Oh." Emma laughs. "Oh, that's perfect. I am going to need all the pictures of that. I will teach my mother not to meddle in my life again."

"Emma," I say. "You're not serious, right? You want the big day. You just said so. A drive-through wedding isn't a big day, babe. It's… it's an afterthought."

"No. Not if we're the ones who plan it. Look, we *could* take back the announcement. We *could* humiliate my mother publicly. Make her look like a fool. And that will certainly teach her a lesson. But the sneakier way to do this is so much better. We get married, she doesn't get to be there—no one gets to be there. Karen Krakken never gets her day on the society page next to Baby Boston and the Bright Berry Beach billionairess, and you know what the best part is?"

I raise my eyebrows at her. "I'm afraid to ask."

"We could be back here in time for Christmas Eve dinner and they would never know." She turns to Miles. "Don't worry. You and Christopher can stay in

Vegas as planned. We'll take a charter back."

"Very well, ma'am. Good plan."

"Good plan? Miles! Dude. This is insanity! Emma is trying to out-boss her bossy mother."

"And then"—Emma is still on a roll—"then… I'm gonna call up the local paper and make them announce our drive-through Vegas wedding. Ha! Merry Christmas, Mom!"

"Emma… let's just take a minute—"

But she's pointing to Miles. "When can we leave?"

"Within the hour, ma'am."

"Perfect. We'll pack and meet you at the airport. Let's do this." And then she turns to me, wraps her arms around my neck, rises up on her tiptoes, kisses me on the mouth, and says, "This will be the most perfect one-up wedding ever!"

I kiss her back, giving in. "I have no doubt, my bossy bride. No doubt at all."

CHAPTER EIGHT

EMMA

Obviously, we have to travel light since this is a stealth mission, but it's no big deal. We don't even need to book a hotel because we're not going to stay over in Vegas. Just land, get hitched in the most outrageous way possible—maybe not an actual drive-through, but for sure something equally ridiculous—and then meet our charter plane back at the airport by eleven AM so we can make it back to Key West for Christmas Eve dinner by eight PM and no one will even know we left.

Take that, Mom. You bossy-buttinski. You think you can out-boss me? Please. I'm the bossiest bosser ever. Even Jesse has to admit that I can out-boss him any day of the week. My mother has nothing on me. Nothing.

Jesse walks out of the bedroom dragging one wheelie carry-on.

"What did you pack?"

"Toothbrushes, makeup, two t-shirts, two pairs of shorts, and my shaving kit."

I stare at him, letting the reality of things sink in fully for a moment. "We're sure?"

"Hey, babe, you're in charge of the wedding. I follow you in all matrimony matters."

"Good answer." I snicker. "OK. So. First, we need to get to the airport." Both of us look out the front window, where the street party is still in full swing. "We can't go that way, obviously." I get out my phone, pull up my Uber app, and then ask for a car. "We'll sneak around back and meet our Uber there. Oh, look! One is just two minutes away! It's like fate!" I press the button to call the car. "Let's go."

We go out through the back yard and leave through the side gate. But it becomes clear that the only way to get over to the street behind us is through Kraken Karen's side yard.

"Shit." I look over my shoulder at the street party. "Do you think the Kraken is still out there? Because we have to sneak past her house."

Jesse looks lazily at the party, then back at me, and shrugs. "Your plan, Ems. I follow you."

I huff. "It would not kill you to be a little bossy, ya know?"

"I don't know where Karen is. But"—he looks past

116

me towards her house—"it's pretty dark in there. I bet they're all at the party. Come on, I'll lead the way since you're terrified of her." He takes my hand and starts pulling me along the fence towards the Krakken back yard.

"I'm not terrified of her," I whisper back as we creep. "I can take Kraken Karen any day of the week."

He shoots a dubious look over his shoulder. "Babe, come on. We're eloping to Vegas in the middle of the night just so you don't have to let her plan your wedding."

"And be my bridesmaid! Anyway, what's your point?"

"My point is… that's kind of ridiculous."

"In a good way though, right?"

"Sure." He chuckles. "In a good way."

Karen's back yard doesn't have a fence, so pretty soon we're over in enemy territory. Then we see the headlights of a slowly creeping car that must surely be our ride come into view and stop in front of the Krakken house. I wasn't paying attention when I called it, so I bet her address popped up once I moved the little marker to one street over.

It's fine though. I'm sure she's still at the party—

"Who's there?"

Shit! Jesse and I stop in our tracks then slowly turn

117

our heads to find a little girl on the back porch. Clearly this is Chauncey Krakken Channing.

"Just us," Jesse says good-naturedly. "Your neighbors. We're meeting that car right there and we'll be—"

"Mom!" the little heathen yells.

"No, no!" Jesse says, dropping my hand and the wheelie handle so he can put both of his up in surrender. "We're just passing through!"

"Mom! Emma Dumas and her boyfriend are creeping around our backyard!"

"Run!" I yell.

Jesse looks at me. "What?"

"Run! Now!"

I take his hand and pull him along the side of Karen's house and when we come out into the front we see the Uber. But it's a few houses up now, looking for us. We dart out into Karen's front yard, trying to head it off before it picks up speed and leaves us behind, when who comes out the front door but—

"Stop right there, Emma!"

And I don't know why, but we do. We stop and turn to look at Karen. She's standing on her front porch with arms crossed. "Where do you think you're going?"

"Vegas," Jesse says.

"What the hell, Jesse? You don't have to tell her!" Then I glare at Karen. "You might think you've weaseled your way back into my life, but you're wrong. You will never, ever"—I'm seething out my words like a crazy woman—"plan my wedding or be my bridesmaid!"

Then I take off in a run, tugging Jesse behind me.

But the car has reached the stop sign at the end of the street and has a blinker on, ready to turn left. "Stop!" I yell. "Here we are!"

Jesse lets go of me and sprints off.

"Stop!" Karen is calling.

I look over my shoulder to find her running after me. I double down and pump my arms, booking it harder to catch up with Jesse.

He's reached the car and is banging on the hood. "We're here!" he's yelling. "It's us."

The Uber car stops in the middle of turning left and Jesse yanks the door open just as I reach him. I slide in, Jesse slides in, and we both say, "Go, go, go!"

The car takes off and I turn to look behind me. Karen is standing in the middle of the road with her phone in her hand. "Oh, my God. I think she's calling my mother!"

"Please!" the driver says. "I don't have any money!"

"What?" Jesse says.

"I don't have any money! Please don't steal my car! I need it for my job!"

Jesse and I both look at each other.

"Oh, shit," I say. Just as the smell of Italian food wafts up to my nose.

"You're not an Uber driver, are you?" Jesse asks.

"Door Dash!" the frightened woman says. "I was making a delivery. I think it was for that lady back there. I was just gonna turn around and—"

"We're just going to the airport," Jesse says. "We'll pay you double to take us there. Hell, we'll pay you two hundred dollars to take us there and pretend this never happened!"

"Do we even have two hundred dollars?" I ask. Because I don't normally carry cash.

The driver pulls over, like she's gonna make us get out, or get out herself, and then we really will have to steal her car, because when I look out the back window, fucking Krakken is running down the street after us, yelling, "They just stole my dinner! They just stole my dinner!"

Well, I can't really *hear* her say that. But I'm pretty sure that's what the Kraken is yelling.

"No, no!" Jesse says. "Please! Don't pull over. This is just a weird misunderstanding. And I do have cash.

I promise." He pauses to look at me. "I do. Only three hundred, but it's fine. We can hit up an ATM in Vegas when we arrive and get more. Just keep going," he tells the driver. "Please. Or crazy Kraken Karen will catch us!"

And maybe it's the word 'kraken' that changes the poor woman's mind, or maybe it's the promise of two hundred dollars. Could go either way. But she gets back on the road and accelerates just as Karen starts pounding on the passenger window.

Jesse and I laugh as we leave the Kraken in the dust. Then we settle back into the seats and breathe a sigh of relief.

"Well," the driver says. I glance up at the rearview to meet her gaze. "I'm gonna need all three hundred of those dollars now. Because I'm pretty sure Karen is already asking to speak to my manager and I'll have an outrageous one-star review before this night is over."

Jesse and I both say, "Done."

At the airport, Jesse gives her all his cash, we thank her and apologize to her simultaneously and profusely, and then we realize he left the wheelie carry-on in Karen's backyard.

"It's fine." Jesse laughs, taking my hand as we make our way through the check-in for the private jets. "We're only going to be in Vegas like six hours. We don't even need toothbrushes."

And pretty soon we're climbing the airstairs to the jet and Miles is making everything better. He even changed back into his butler outfit.

"Miles," I say, tsking my tongue. "You didn't have to change."

"Ma'am, I take my job very seriously. Looking the part makes me a better butler. Mr. Boston, will you require some Barbie and Ken mini rolls during our trip?"

"Nah, I'm good, Miles. Take the night off. In fact, you can have the bedroom if you want. We'll just sleep in our seats."

"I wouldn't dream of it," Miles snaps back. "And I already have your sleeping clothes laid out for you."

"We have sleeping clothes?" Jesse asks.

"I procured them from the jet lounge concierge while we were fueling up."

Jesse smiles at me. "I love your butler."

"Would you like some tips for getting married in Vegas, ma'am?"

"Well…" I look at Jesse and he shrugs. "Sure, I guess. Do you have much experience in Vegas weddings?"

"I've done it twice myself," Miles says with a straight face.

Jesse leans forward and pats the seat across from us. "Sit, Miles. You're off the clock. Tell us everything you know about getting hitched in Vegas."

So Miles sits and starts talking.

He tells us all about our options, and who knew that the drive-through wedding isn't even the most outrageous way to tie the knot in Vegas?

You can get married while sky-diving. "If you book online, they give you the tourist package. But if you know who to talk to, they will recite your actual nuptials fourteen thousand feet in the air. It's a tandem jump," he explains. "But they will give you mic-enabled helmets and situate you so that you and Jesse can hold hands and say 'I do' while you fall towards Earth going two hundred feet per second."

"Wow," Jesse says. Then he looks at me. "That's pretty outrageous."

"What else can we do?" I ask, not sold on the whole falling-from-the-sky wedding.

"There's always the underwater wedding."

"Oh, shit!" Jesse points to Miles and snaps his fingers. "That's perfect!" He looks at me, excited like a kid at Christmas. "Right? Dumas Diving! Vegas style!"

"That would really piss my mother off." I snicker. "But what else? Because getting married underwater sounds like something my mother might actually be into."

"There's the Elvis wedding, of course. With optional showgirls as bridesmaids. I did that once when I married John."

"John, huh?" I wink at Miles. "Who was the other guy?"

"The other one was Cynthia. She was an actual showgirl, and since her life was nothing but glitz and glam from top to bottom, she wanted something more traditional. So we did the skydive."

"John and Cynthia," Jesse muses. "You're an enigma, Miles."

"That I am, sir. But there are many other ways to do a Vegas wedding right. You can even have a real ceremony in one of the five-star hotels."

"Doesn't that require things like… planning?" Jesse asks. "I mean, I'm sure they're all booked up. It is Christmas Eve."

"I have connections, sir," Miles says. And he's not even smug about it. Just very matter-of-fact. *I have connections.*

"Wow," I say. "I don't know. There seems to be a lot of choices."

"Which is good, right?" Jesse says. "We want all the choices. Isn't that what you were talking about earlier? You want to pick the dress, and the flowers, and the cake and all that shit."

"Yeah."

"So…" Jesse looks at Miles. "We want that. All the choices."

"Very well, sir. I have a man called Fingers. He's the most sought-after wedding planner in Vegas, ten years running. He plans very unique, custom-tailored wedding experiences. And he owes me a favor. So I'm sure he will be happy to help."

"Fingers, huh?" Jesse chuckles. "Any relation to Shoes?"

"None, sir."

"OK." Jesse looks at me. "What do you say? Should we go with Fingers and let him make the plans?"

"Why not?" I laugh. "Seems very Vegas to have a man called Fingers planning your outrageous on-the-run elopement."

CHAPTER NINE

JESSE

Miles insists that we change into our silky new PJs and take the jet bedroom while he makes some phone calls to Fingers, assuring us that everything will be all set by the time we land.

And even though I have big plans for seducing my bride-to-be while we're in the air, we're both kinda exhausted when we finally snuggle under the covers and turn out the lights. Add in the low, white-noise hum of the engines and… yeah. I'm pretty much asleep immediately.

But it feels like I only just closed my eyes when Miles is gently shaking me awake and offering me a lemon-scented hand towel to freshen up.

"We'll be landing in about twenty minutes, sir. I've taken the liberty of steaming the wrinkles out of yesterday's clothes and they are hanging in the closet."

"Jesus, Miles. You're one in a million, ya know that?"

"I do, sir."

It's nearly dawn when I finally drag myself up out of bed and open the window shade to look outside. The barren terrain of desert greets me down below and our plan suddenly seems a lot crazier than it did last night.

Emma covers her mouth as she yawns. "What time is it?"

"Almost six AM. Miles left you a hot lemon towel."

"God, I love Miles." Emma swings her legs out of bed and gazes out the window for a moment. "Holy shit. We're really doing this."

"We really are."

She looks at me. "Are we nuts?"

"Uh… yeah. That's a given. Especially after that whole Krakken chase last night."

Emma snorts. "Take that, *Karen*."

"Are you sure you want to do this?"

"What do you mean?"

"Emma. It's your wedding. You only get to do it once."

"Unless your name is Miles." She chuckles.

"You know what I mean. This is supposed to be your day."

"It is my day. I'm excited." She pouts at me. God, I still love that pout. "But if you're not into it—"

"No, no. I am. I'm up for any crazy wedding you can cook up. But… I just want to make sure this is what you really want. Because we could just go back home, talk things out with your mother like rational people—"

"She's the irrational one! How could she invite Karen to be my wedding planner-slash-bridesmaid? I mean, come on! She knows that Mila, Nat, and Hannah have been my besties for over a decade now. That's like… unforgivable." She points her finger at me. "And I know what you're going to say."

"What am I gonna say?"

"That she only wants what's best for me. But seriously. This is my mother we're talking about. Sure, she loves me. But she's always trying to control me. And you give in to her."

"When?"

"All the time!"

"Name one time."

"Hello? Have we or have we not been flying to Key West for Saturday dinner every freaking week?"

"We did miss that one time in September."

"Yeah, once! And that month had five Saturdays instead of four, so it was a bonus dinner! And she forced my whole family to drive up to the city in the freaking Suburban!"

"And I did tell her I wanted to come when we first met."

"Twice a month! Not every week. See, this is what I mean. She makes all these reasonable offers like, 'Would you like first and third Saturdays, Jesse? Or second and fourth?'"

"And I chose second and third. See? I made my own plan."

"She wants you to think that, but it's not true. Not even a little bit! Second and third turned into every week. That was her plan all along."

"You make her sound like a sneaky buttinski mother-in-law."

"She is! Mark my words. When my mother makes a plan, she makes a freaking plan. I'm talking plan A, B, C, D all the way to Z. And each plan is worked and reworked so that no matter what road you take to get to the end, it always turns out the way she wants it to."

I laugh at her.

"It's not funny!"

"OK, your mother is some crime-family matron who has all the power and will send in her henchmen to get what she wants. Got it."

"No! That's me! I'm the crime-family matron

now!"

"Oh, Emma."

"Stop looking at me like I'm ridiculous! I'm telling you, she's plotting my wedding so that no matter what I do, it will end up the way she wants it. I've been through this all before. Ask me about prom night!"

I'm not gonna ask her about prom night for two reasons. One, I'll get jealous no matter how it turns out. And two, I need to talk her down off this ledge she's on before things really go off the rails. We were very close to being charged with carjacking last night. And we did steal the Kraken's Italian Christmas Eve eve dinner. So I say, "Well… not anymore, right?"

She sighs. "Right. This is the perfect plan. I'm telling you. The look on her face when I tell her we eloped and it's a done deal—that's my Christmas present this year. That's all I want."

"To foil your mother's wedding plans?"

"Yup."

"OK, babe. Then get ready for your present. Because that sound right there?" I point to the floor where we can hear the landing gear being released. "That's Santa's sleigh coming in for a landing."

We take our seats in the main cabin and Miles serves us coffee and mini rolls to munch on while we land. Then we go back into the bedroom and put on yesterday's refreshed clothes. Once that's done, we exit and meet Miles at the bottom of the jet stairs.

Vegas isn't as hot as Key West was, but it's still pretty nice when we finally get out in the sun and turn to Miles, eager to hear what our plans are.

He hands me a glossy black mini-folder and says, "Here is your itinerary."

I open it up to find the charter jet scheduled for our return trip, the details for the car that will take us to our first meeting with Fingers, and a hundred dollars cash.

"For any incidentals you need until you can get to an ATM," Miles explains.

God, I love this dude. He thinks of everything. When I'm in Miles' capable hands, everything is right in the world.

"But," Emma interjects, taking the little folder from my hands, "there are no wedding plans in here. Just the car and the plane."

"Fingers will have all those details for you when you meet him at the restaurant," Miles says. "I hope you both have the Vegas wedding of your dreams and I'll see you after New Year's."

"Thank you, Miles," Emma coos, then kisses him on the cheek.

"Merry Christmas, ma'am."

I stuff the little folder into my back pocket, take Emma's hand, and head off across the tarmac with a smile.

It's not every day you get to marry your soulmate in an impromptu Vegas elopement planned by a dude called Fingers.

I'm pretty sure this will be the most exciting day of my life.

Finding the driver after leaving security is easy. He's a big guy in a black suit and sunglasses holding a digital sign that says 'Boston Wedding.'

Nice touch, Miles. Nice touch.

Since we don't have any luggage, we just follow him to the pick-up lane and get in the back of a black Lincoln Navigator. The temperature is perfect, the leather seats are luxuriously butter-soft, and there are two bottles of Fiji water chilling in an ice bucket.

Emma and I look at each other, smiling.

"This is gonna be great," she says.

"Fuckin' perfect. I can just tell. Fingers has it all

figured out."

"What do you think he looks like?"

"Fingers? Uh... I imagine he's missing a few."

"What?"

"Yeah, like the name? It's gotta be ironic, right? That's the only way it works."

"He sounds like a gangster." Emma chuckles.

"He so does. But fuckin' Miles? He's sorta gangster so that fits."

"Miles? What are you talking about?"

"You know. His whole seedy Pittsburgh past with that guy called Shoes."

"What?"

"Yeah. He's here because of his Mob-nurtured Rain Man abilities."

"What. The hell. Are you talking about?"

"He never told you about his childhood? Growing up with the Mob?"

Emma guffaws so loud, our driver checks on us in the rearview. "No. This is a joke, right?"

"I don't think so. Dude told me this whole long story about how he was like an orphan or some shit back in Pittsburgh and got shuffled off to a Mob boss in Chicago and then bought his way out and went to butler school and found your ad on the *Modern Butler* magazine website and that's how he got here."

She's laughing so hard by the time I stop talking, I can't help but laugh with her. "What? Was he lying to me?"

"Jesse." She can't stop laughing.

"What? It sounded so reasonable."

"*Modern Butler?*"

"Everyone needs trade publications. Hell, I used to get a magazine called *Douche Yacht High Life* when I was younger."

She's still laughing.

"They just send it to you when you… never mind." I huff and look out the window. "So what's his real story then? If that was all a lie."

"I don't know. But it wasn't *that*."

"You don't know then." I huff again. "I think he was telling the truth. And look, the wedding planner is called Fingers. It has to be true. Miles showed us that crazy map of how he had to get to the poker tournament tonight, remember?"

"I wasn't really paying attention, but OK. Fine." Emma stops me with a hand on my shoulder. "You win. Miles is Mob. Got it."

"He is," I insist. "I can smell a lie." I point at her. "And that story wasn't a lie. Why would Miles lie to me? He totally laughs at my jokes. Dude *gets* me."

She's still chuckling, but she's polite enough to do

it behind a hand over her mouth. "You're adorable."

I adjust the collar of my t-shirt. "Thank you."

But I'm still kinda miffed at Miles when we land at Big Mike's. The jukebox is playing *Sugar, Sugar* and the whole place looks like a Fifties diner.

A hostess on roller skates dressed up in a classic pink uniform rolls her way over to a table and pans her hand at it.

We sit together on the same side of the booth, expecting Fingers to show up and sit across from us.

"Would you like to order?" a friendly gum-chewing waitress asks, also on roller skates.

"Should we eat?" Emma asks.

"Why not? Godfather Miles did give us some spending money."

She laughs at me again.

I'm gonna kill Miles for this.

We order the breakfast buffet, fill up our plates with hash browns and bacon, and then lean back and scan the parking lot outside, trying to figure out if any of the approaching patrons of Big Mike's could be Fingers. We're both pointing at a skinny dude wearing white fingerless gloves and a purple pimp hat, certain that's him, when a guy slips into our booth and says, "You must be the Bostons," as he holds up a phone with a picture of us sleeping on the jet bed on the screen.

Which is super creepy, but not wholly unexpected at this point.

"That's us." Emma beams. "And you must be Fingers."

"No, no, no." The guy laughs. "No, I'm Clarence. Fingers is the big boss. I'm the wedding point man."

I squint my eyes at him. "You don't look like a wedding point man." He's wearing a cowboy hat and smells like mint chewing tobacco.

He smiles broadly at me. Lotsa teeth. "Keep people on their toes. That's our motto. 'Weddings that keep you on your toes.'"

"Hosted by Fingers." Emma beams.

I shake my head and shoot her a look that says, *No, babe. Not now. Cowboy here looks unstable.*

But Cowboy Clarence takes it all in stride and says. "So, what kind of wedding were you envisioning? Hmm? Five-star hotel with a mani-pedi package and a wedding party of thirty?" He winks after getting all that out. Like it's a joke.

"No," I say, narrowing my eyes at him. "We're only here for like five more hours. Just a quick, super-spontaneous, super-ridiculous elopement wedding so we can teach her mother a lesson."

He snaps his fingers and points at me. "Ferris

wheel?"

"Maybe." I shrug.

"Dude ranch?"

"Is that a thing?" Emma asks, hopefully.

"Sure. We can make anything happen, sweetheart. Anything you want. Fingers is your man."

"Maybe not a dude ranch. Learning how to ride sounds time-consuming. Something fast. We really do have to be back in Key West for Christmas Eve dinner."

"Mother-in-law got you by the balls, huh?"

"No," I say.

But Emma says, "Oh, yeah, she does. Got him good too. She says jump, he jumps."

"I do not. Do you have like…a menu? Or something that spells it all out for us? We're not sure what we want, but we'll know it when we see it."

Cowboy clicks his tongue at us like we're ponies and points his finger like a gun. "I got you." Then he whips a brochure out of his back pocket and slaps it on the table. "Take a good long gander at this. I'm gonna go rustle me up a breakfast burrito at the counter. BRB."

He gets up and heads towards the counter as Emma and I look dubiously at the crinkled, wrinkled, is-that-a-coffee-stain?, used-up, tri-fold brochure he left behind.

We side-eye each other and laugh.

"Still game?" Emma asks.

"Hey, I'm in. Let's do it."

I pick up the brochure by the corner edge and flip it open.

"'Welcome to Fingers' Fantasy Weddings. Where we keep you on your toes,'" Emma reads.

I just shake my head. Because I can't.

"Oh, look. Here's a picture of the underwater wedding at the aquarium. That really does sound like us, don't you think?"

"Yeah. It does. But this is our *one* wedding. Do we really want to be *us*?"

"Oh, fuck. I don't think we can, anyway. You need to show proof of SCUBA certification." She eyeballs me. "We can't exactly call home and have my dad email them over, right?"

"Probably not. But look, here's a rollercoaster wedding. That sounds fun."

"Skydiving is kinda cool."

"And terrifying," I add. I mean… I'm not gonna come right out and say it, but falling out of a plane doesn't sound like the best way to start your new married life, if you ask me.

"I don't know. Maybe a little adrenaline rush is

what we need?"

"How about this one?" I laugh. "Shotgun wedding at Red Mesa Resort! Look, they're all dressed up like gangsters."

"Maybe that's where Miles moonlights on his days off?" Emma quips.

"OK, OK. He was lying. Fine."

I'm so gonna kill Miles the next time I see him. I really thought we were friends.

Cowboy Clarence slips back into the booth chewing on a breakfast burrito. "So. Make up your minds?" He winks at my almost-bride.

"Not yet," I say.

"We like a bunch of them. We're just not sure which one."

"We only get to do this once," I add. "It's kind of a big deal."

Clarence puts up both hands. "I get it. Totally get it. And it's your lucky day. Because here at Finger's Fantasy Weddings we get *you*." He points to us like this is all part of the act. "That's why we offer the Ultimate Fingers' Fantasy Wedding Buffet."

"Buffet?" Emma and I both say.

"It's like a… pick three. Except you don't get to pick 'em. We do. And we rustle you around town and by the end of the day you've had yourself three incredible, one-of-a-kind Fingers' Fantasy Weddings."

Emma shoots him with her finger. "That keep you on your toes!"

"You betcha!" He laughs, clearly enamored with my girl.

Emma looks at me. "What do you think?"

I shrug. "It's your day, babe. I go where you go."

"OK," she says, almost breathless. "We're in. Fingers' Fantasy Wedding Pick Three Buffet it is."

"All right then," Clarence says. "Here's what's gonna happen. You're gonna give me your credit card, I'm gonna run it on my little PayPal app here on my phone for a grand total of five thousand dollars, and then I'm gonna walk on over to that pay phone right there and make some arrangements with Fingers while I finish up my burrito. You good people will sit tight over here and eat up." He points to us again. "You're gonna need that energy. I'm about to rustle up the best day of your life, so you better grab seconds. And then we'll get 'er done!"

"Let's get 'er done!" Emma squeals. "Give him the credit card, Jesse!"

I hand it to him and Clarence tips his hat to Emma while he takes it. Then he slides out of the booth and walks across the restaurant where the pay phone must be.

"Wow," I say. "This place is really something."

"Right?" Emma laughs. "I knew this was a good idea last night, but in the bright light of day, it's even better. We're about to have an amazing day, I can just tell."

And it does feel like a pretty special day. I mean… how often can you possibly expect to go to sleep in Key West, wake up in Vegas, meet with Cowboy Clarence, and buy Fingers' Fantasy Wedding Pick Three Buffet in less than twelve hours?

Once.

This is a once-in-a-lifetime experience all the way around.

But twenty minutes later, when I get up to use the restroom and ask where the pay phone is, the friendly waitress on skates tells me there is no pay phone.

And no Cowboy Clarence, either.

He's gone.

And he took my credit card.

CHAPTER TEN

"That's impossible," I tell Jesse as I follow him outside to look for the cowboy. "He was too nice to rob us."

"Emma," Jesse says, spinning around to face me in the parking lot. "This is Vegas. We had a meeting with a guy called Fingers to set up our crazy wedding and some dude called Clarence waltzed in and we just said, 'Oh, OK. He must be the fuckin' Thumb. It's all good. Yes, we'd like the Pick Three Wedding Buffet Package and why, sure, you can have my credit card.' What did we think was gonna happen here?"

"I know. I get it. We're kinda dumb. But I still have this really good feeling about him. It's probably a misunderstanding."

"A misunderstanding? He said, word for word, 'You good people will sit tight over here and eat up while I *rob* you!'"

"That's *not* what he said."

"He might as well have! And look!" Jesse pans his arms wide as he spins in the middle of the parking lot. "He's gone!"

"Well… that's stupid. What a jerk. But I still can't believe that Miles would set us up with some weird Vegas wedding swindlers."

"He was in the Mob, Emma!"

"Oh, stop it! He was not in the Mob, Jesse. He grew up in Philly and went to an elite private school. The man has a PhD in manners, for fuck's sake. And he invented the Barbie and Ken mini-cinnamon roll. He's *not* in the damn Mob!"

Jesse points to himself. "I went to an elite private school and *I'm* in the fuckin' Mob!"

I laugh. I can't help it. "Yeah, but—"

"Yeah, but nothing. Which one of those stories he told seems more likely now, huh?"

I roll my eyes. "You're not in the Mob. You're in the—"

"Something worse!" he says. "Worse than the Mob. So much worse we're not even sure what it is! For all we know, we're being set up by *my* Mob!"

"Now you're really starting to lose it. Let's just go back inside, eat the rest of our bacon, and wait it out.

I'm sure he'll be back."

Jesse sucks in a deep breath, holds it for like five whole seconds, and then lets it out in a rush. "Fine." He throws up his hands. "Fine. What other choice do we have? After I pay for the fuckin' breakfast buffet with my butler allowance we'll have just enough to Uber back to the airport and wait for our charter."

"What? No! We came here to get married. We're getting married. We don't need cash. We have credit cards. We're billionaires, for fuck's sake. We don't have to go back to the airport—"

My phone dings in my purse. I fish it out and then hold up a finger. "Hold, please. This is Miles." I accept the call and say, "Hey, Miles, so that guy... Oh, yes." I smile at Jesse as he makes that gimme-the-phone gesture with his fingers, then turn my back and plug one ear so I can hear. "Yes. We're still here... Oh. OK. Sure. Thanks! And have a good time on your break... yup. Merry Christmas to you too, Miles. Byeeee!"

When I turn back to Jesse he has his arms crossed over his chest and is tapping his foot on the cracked blacktop. "Well?"

"That was Miles."

"Obviously. What did he say? And where the hell is my credit card? Do I need to report it stolen?"

"What? No. Jesus. Turns out Clarence was just the

Thumb."

"Do not—"

"Kidding. But only sorta. Clarence did say he was only the point man. Miles says we have to go back inside so we can pick our cake and flowers."

"What?"

"See? I told you everything was fine. Talk about overreacting. I wish I had that rant on video. It was classic Jesse Boston."

"He really said that?"

"I swear to God. They called him wondering where we went. They're all waiting for us inside. I guess Big Mike's is the first stop on our Magical Mystery Wedding Tour."

Jesse doesn't look completely convinced, but he finally just shrugs. "OK. Let's do this."

He takes my hand and leads me back inside and… "Holy crap. Where did everyone go?"

"Oh, we close early when we get a Pick Three Buffet order, Emma," the roller-skating hostess says. "Just follow me and we'll get started on the cake-testing. I don't want to rush you, but I know you folks are in a hurry to catch a plane. So we've got everything set up already."

And wow. Do they ever. There are literally two dozen tiny cakes to test. All laid out on a shimmery gold table cloth that looks like it used to be a showgirl in its former life.

"Have a seat and we'll start bringing them over."

I smile at Jesse. "See? This is good, right? All these cakes to test." I shrug my shoulders up to my ears and make a little squeal.

He smiles at me. "OK. You were right. I overreacted."

"I don't care. Come on. Let's eat cake!"

We sit and they bring us two tiny slices at a time. We taste German chocolate with a cherry cream filling, carrot cake with peach-flavored cream-cheese frosting, a lemon cake with layers of sliced strawberries, and there's even one called Bavarian ice cream.

And they are all wonderful.

Like I don't know who's back there in Big Mike's kitchen baking up tiny wedding cake samples, but whoever it is, they are obviously a culinary genius.

"So which one?" I ask Jesse, once we've tasted them all. Our table is littered with tiny plates and leftover bites.

He holds up a finger, tastes them all again, and then points to the lemon strawberry. "I love that one."

"Me too!" I turn to the roller hostess and say, "We'll take that one."

"Excellent choice, Mrs. Boston."

And oh, that makes me squeal. Mrs. Fucking. Boston. How long have I dreamed of that? It hits me then. "I'm really going to be your wife!"

Jesse takes my hand and kisses my knuckles. "You really are, Mrs. Boston."

CHAPTER ELEVEN

The Big Mike's people start bringing out flower arrangements and books of bouquet pictures and suddenly I'm having a conversation about baby's breath and whether or not Emma should choose the peonies over the roses, or the roses over the peonies.

"How about both?" I say, and Emma beams at me. "It's your day, babe. Get whatever you want. All the peonies and all the roses."

"What color do you like Jesse?" Emma holds the book of color combinations open between us so I can get a good look.

Jesus. I don't care. But I don't say that. My bride deserves the dream wedding. Sure, we're eloping and our wedding coordinator is a guy called Fingers, but that doesn't mean we have to skimp. So I offer up an opinion of, "Yellow. And peach."

"Oh, I love that combination too."

"Then it's settled." I look up at the flower coordinator. "Give her everything she wants."

Emma giggles and leans into my shoulder and everything kinda hits me all at once.

It's real.

This is real. We really ran from Key West. We really are in Vegas. We really are getting married... today.

To. Day.

Tonight, Emma will be my wife. The honeymoon starts tonight!

I wonder if our wedding package includes lingerie?

A small, pale, professionally-dressed woman appears, whisking away the flower people hovering around us. She points to the table and then orders it to be cleared of cake tasting plates in a cool, but maybe a little frightening, Russian accent.

People jump to do as she says, and then the little lady claps her hands three times and...

Roller-skating waitresses have now been transformed into wedding-dress models. They skate in, the long trains of their gowns trailing out behind them, and then turn, hold hands, and skate in roughly the shape of a circle with hands in the middle. They shout, "One, two, three, BRIDE!" like this is a 'go team' chant on a football field, and then they spin backwards and flip up on their toe stops with hands in the air in a grand 'tada' gesture, like they just dismounted off the uneven bars at the Olympics.

Emma applauds. "Oh, my God, that was amazing!" She looks at me, still clapping like crazy. "This is the best wedding plan ever."

The little dress lady says, "You pick dress now. I make it," in her scary Russian accent.

"OK!" Emma says, still very excited.

"But… should I be here for this?" I ask. "It's supposed to be a surprise?"

"It will be surprise," the dress lady says, nodding her head. She calls out, "Machine!" and Emma and I jump a little at how loud such a little person can be. But then we laugh. Because the hostess skates out with a sewing machine on a wheeled table.

"I make custom," the dressmaker says. "She pick favorite style, I sew up. You see later, bossy man."

"Right here?" Emma says, looking at me with a huge grin. Like this whole thing is so crazy. "In the restaurant?"

"This not restaurant. This Big Mike's."

"OK!" Emma's clearly on board with that illogical explanation.

"Wow," I say, looking at my watch. It's already almost eight o'clock. "But we have to be back on the plane by eleven. Is the dress gonna be ready in time?"

"Time, no problem. Take twenty minutes."

"Twenty minutes?" Emma exclaims, looking at me all flushed pink with delight. "You're pretty fast!"

"You pick style now. I make fancy dress for you." And then she snaps her fingers and the roller-skating models start another routine.

I have to admit, none of these dresses are very spectacular. They're all a little bit ragged. And the trains are kinda dirty from being dragged across the floor. And yeah, if this is only going to take twenty minutes… I'm not convinced what Emma ends up with will be anything amazing.

But Emma doesn't seem to notice. And even if the dress isn't amazing, it will still be special. Because from what I've seen so far, this Fingers dude, he's definitely cornered the market on fantasy Vegas elopement weddings.

The whole fuckin' thing is insane.

Emma gets up and starts looking over all the dresses. The dressmaker snaps her fingers again and a whole team of women appear with measuring tapes and start measuring Emma while she points to various elements she likes.

Another team works on my measurements and there's lot of talk about buttons, and lace, and chiffon, and bodices, which is all a little bit boring. But then I hear 'garters.' And 'corset.' And 'stockings.'

I can get on board with that.

Except... this is kinda taking a while. The next time I look at my watch it's nearly nine o'clock.

I walk over to Emma. "Hey, babe."

"Oh, this dress, Jesse. Oh, my God. You're gonna love it."

"I already do. But... it's getting late. I don't understand how we're gonna do three weddings in two hours. It doesn't seem possible." I direct my apprehension towards the stoic dressmaker. She ignores me. So I say, "Excuse me. Do you know when we'll be... you know, getting this show on the road?"

She shakes her head, pins in her mouth as she fusses with one of the roller-brides' dresses. "Not my department." Then she juts her chin at something behind me.

I look over my shoulder and see a tall, thin man wearing a faded red polo shirt waving his fingers at me. His blond hair is clearly combed over a large bald patch on top of his head and he's chewing on a toothpick like a moment hasn't gone by in the past fifteen years where he didn't have a toothpick in his mouth. It dangles for a second, then his tongue flips it over to the other side of his mouth, and it bounces between his lips to the beat of *Under the Boardwalk* playing on the jukebox.

I walk over to him. "Are you one of the Thumbs?" Which I realize is an inside joke between Emma and I, but it must not be original, because he gets it.

"Yes." He laughs. "I'm Steve, your Fingers' Fantasy Wedding Pick Three Buffet coordinator number one. Are we almost ready here? Or does your *bee-u-tee-ful* bride-to-be need a few more minutes?"

"Yeah, ah… I think so. Emma? I'm not trying to rush you, but"—I tap my watch—"it's getting late. We wanna make sure we get the full wedding experience."

"Full wedding experience coming your way," Steve assures me.

"OK, OK, OK," Emma says. Then she points to something else on the dress and turns to walk over to us with her shoulders all bunched up to her ears, wide toothy grin on her face.

I take her hand and give it a squeeze.

"You are one lucky man," Steve says.

"Don't I know it."

"OK." Steve rubs his hands together so fast I almost fear he'll spark up a fire from the friction. "Let's do this! Your chariot awaits!"

He pans his hand at the window to a sparkly lavender van. On the side panel, in large fancy script font, it says "Fingers' Fantasy Weddings" and there's a picture of a cheesy car-salesman-type dude—presumably Fingers—making a heart with his fingers. And nope. I can count ten of them, so he's not missing any.

Emma and I look at each other and shake our heads.

"OK," I say. "Let's go."

Emma looks over at the dressmaker. She's already sitting down at the machine, barking orders at everyone as they bring her fabric and lace. "But… what about my dress?"

Steve smiles even bigger, his toothpick still bouncing on his lips. "The dress is for the last wedding. That's the special one. The first two are just a taste of what could have been."

Emma nods like this makes sense. "Ah. OK. We're in your capable hands, Steve."

And can I just say? I love her optimism. I'm pretty sure this whole thing is gonna be a disaster—I mean, it hasn't been planned, none of our family will be here, and the whole setup is ridiculous—but she believes.

And because of that… I decide to believe too.

We go outside and Steve swings the side door of the van open with a flourish that would make Vanna White jealous. And inside it is what can only be described as tricked out.

I'm talking full-on Seventies fuck-truck kind of tricked out, complete with purple and pink shag carpet that's so long you can probably comb it, a pink leather loveseat, a bar, and yup—no Seventies porn van is complete without a bed in the back. There's even a canopy of purple mosquito netting hanging above it, just in case you feel the need to consummate your marriage on the road.

Emma barks out a laugh.

But we get in. Steve closes the door with a *thunk*, and then a few moments later he's in the driver's seat and we're on our way. "First stop, New York, New York, folks! Rollercoaster wedding, here we come!"

"Yay!" Emma claps. "You wanted to do that one, right?"

"Sounds fun, right?"

"So much fun. This is gonna be the best day ever!"

We settle in on the couch, swaying back and forth as Steve takes tight corners over to the Strip and the New York, New York Hotel. Emma is still smiling, but quieter now.

"What's up?" I ask. Because I can tell when her mood is shifting.

"Nothing's up. Why do you ask?"

"Because thirty seconds ago you were squealing and now your eyebrows are crinkling."

"I'm super excited. We're getting married, Jesse!"

"I know. And you got to pick the cake, and the flowers, and you're getting a one-of-a-kind Fingers' Fantasy Wedding custom dress."

She sighs. "It's pretty cool. I'm actually having a lot of fun. And I know the dress will just be parts of other dresses repurposed, but... it's still a nice touch."

"But..." I say.

"But... I wish Natalie, and Hannah, and Mila were here, ya know?"

"We can just go home. Just have our regularly scheduled wedding next spring."

"And give in to my mother's diabolical plan?" She huffs. "With Kraken Karen up on the altar with us? No thank you."

"I kinda wish Johnny and Joey were here too. We'd probably tear this town up with a Boston bachelor party."

"Oh, my God. You guys so would. And Huck and Wald. And Darrel—"

"Who's Darrel?"

"Hannah's boyfriend."

"Oh. I just call him what's-his-name."

"And Diego, and whichever two or three boys Natalie brings as her dates."

"If that's what you want, Emma, we can do that."

"No. We're here. We're in the middle of the best day of our lives. A day we'll *never* forget. Just think of the stories we'll have to tell when this is over!"

"Yeah." I chuckle. "That's for sure. It's already pretty unorthodox. I can only imagine it gets crazier from here. I mean, roller skates?"

Emma giggles. "I sorta love my dressmaker. She's so... mean."

"Fuckin' little Russian ladies. You really can't hate them."

"Twenty minutes though?"

"Yeah. We'll see. But... Steve did say that the dress is for the last wedding, so I'm sure it will be fine."

I'm a little bit stressed about the time factor. Because this is fun and crazy and all, but my almost-mother-in-law will not forgive me if I don't deliver her daughter for Christmas Eve dinner.

But then Steve takes another tight corner and Emma slides into me. And I make the most of the opportunity by kissing her. It's a nice, soft, easy kiss that immediately relaxes me. I let all the worry go and just trust in... fate, I guess. Trust that the universe knows what it's doing and this day will be perfect.

He slams on the brakes and we crash together, laughing. OK, so this whole thing is pretty... eh, trashy? Maybe? But... it is fun. I kinda feel like this is

158

the plot of the next *Christmas Vacation* movie. It has a decent setup for that, for sure.

The van door swings open and an older woman with short gray hair smiles brightly at us. "Welcome to the New York, New York Hotel and Casino! Please come with me for your fabulous Fingers Wedding experience!"

Emma takes a deep breath. "Ready?"

And you know what?

I am ready.

So ready to make this woman my wife.

I grab her hand and help her out of the van. The greeter says, "Follow me, please. We have to hurry. The ceremony is about to start."

Oh, good. I don't want to rush us or anything. But we really don't have a lot of time here. We walk fast and Greeter Grandma leads us past the reception desk and over to the elevators. We get in, go up to the second floor, and then head on over to the Big Apple Coaster.

There's a wedding party already there. Bride, groom, etc, etc. Everybody chatting and excited about the big upcoming moment. But no one else. It's only then that I notice the coaster isn't even open yet. This is all being done before operating hours.

Emma squeezes my hand. "Oh, my God. I'm

nervous. Are you nervous?"

"Little bit," I admit. But then I look at her and shake my head. "Nah. I'm not nervous. I can't wait."

Grandma and one of the coaster workers walk over to the wedding party and a hushed, but heated discussion starts.

"What's going on?" Emma asks.

"I dunno."

Then all of them look over at us. Several people are frowning.

"Shit, what's happening, Jesse?"

But then it's pretty clear what's happening. Because a strap of cash appears in Grandma's hand. She waves it in front of the bride and groom and their annoyed expressions turn to surprise.

They look at us again, then down at the money, then at each other.

The bride takes the neat strap of cash into her hand, which I can deduce is probably either five thousand dollars, if the notes are fifties, or ten thousand dollars, if the notes are hundreds.

Either way, it's a lot of tax-free cash and I suddenly wonder how much Fingers charges for his fantasy weddings.

Clarence still has my credit card.

But I don't have any more time to think about that

because the bride nods, stuffs the strap into her bra, and Grandma turns and waves us forward.

"OK, Fugosi family wedding party!" an organizer shouts. "We're this way! Follow me!"

I glance at Grandma, but she's already walking off.

"What do we do?" Emma asks.

"Uh… follow the wedding party, I guess."

So that's what we do. We follow them back to the coaster line-up and end up on the station platform. The Fugosis are being ushered into the waiting train that's painted up to look like a yellow cab in New York City, bride and groom in the front car, and then a worker points to us and the seat directly behind the bride and groom.

"Here goes nothing," Emma squeals, as she climbs in and takes a seat.

I get in, and then suddenly everything is happening very fast. The restraint harnesses are slammed down by a large man with a long beard. Then he hands Emma and I a pair of wraparound earbuds and points to his ears. "Put them on," he says. "That's how you hear the wedding."

"Got it," I say, adjusting my earbuds.

Emma does the same and then there's a voice in my ears. "Karen and Chad!" the tinny voice says. "Are you ready for the first day of the rest of your life?"

The wedding party cheers. But Emma is grabbing my arm. "What the fuck? Karen and Chad?"

"Yeah, that's weird, babe."

She looks around. "Is this some kind of joke?"

But clearly there *is* a Karen and Chad, and they are dressed up like bride and groom, so... "I think it's real. Just... a very weird coincidence."

She opens her mouth to say something, but then the train is moving forward and the—

reverend? Priest? Wedding official?—begins the ceremony with, "We are gathered here together to celebrate the union of Karen and Chad..."

Emma and I look at each other and shrug as we approach the first hill and start climbing. Fuck it. We knew this was just the practice run and we have two more chances to get married after this, so who cares if we're coaster-bombing the Fugosi wedding?

"Chad, do you promise to love and cherish Karen? Through the highs and lows, through the good and the bad?"

We reach the top of the hill and there's a moment of high expectations and jittery silence before the announcer continues, "Through sickness and health, for as long as you live, or until you die on the Big Apple Coaster?"

I laugh. Fucking Vegas.

And then we're going down and everyone is screaming, and I'm not even sure Chad is on board with his marriage vows, but who cares?

We come off the first hill and the announcer is talking again. "And Karen. Lovely Karen. No, you cannot speak to my manager about my inappropriate wedding vows. Do you, Karen—"

The coaster whips us to the side and I lose a few moments of the vows.

But then his voice is there again as we jerk back and forth towards another hill. "—for as long as you live, or until Chad cheats on you with a showgirl down in the casino, loses all the bribe money you just took to allow Jesse and Emma to take the place of your bridesmaid and best man, and you hire a hitman to off him?"

We go upside down and everyone is screaming again, so no clue if Karen's on board either.

But when I look over at Emma she's smiling and squealing with delight. And that's all I care about.

"Everyone!" the announcer says. "Put your hands in the air and scream, 'I do!'"

Everyone does. Including Emma and I.

The announcer keeps the ceremony going but I'm too busy being jerked around and laughing to hear anything else until we finally slow down and approach the station.

"I now pronounce you husband and wife!" the officiator shouts. And then he morphs into his legal disclaimer voice and starts talking real fast. "Please do not attempt to exit the train until the ride has come to a complete stop. New York, New York Hotel and Casino takes no responsibility for your marriage contract. This is not a legally binding ceremony until your wedding documents have been signed and filed. Have a nice life and if you need a quickie annulment, please visit Marty. L. Mitts in Twain Swenson Plaza, ten minutes northeast of the casino! Congratulations, Chad and Karen!"

The train car jerks to a stop and the safety harnesses release.

I stand up, my legs shaky and my head a little dizzy from the ride. And Emma is taking my hand. "Oh, my God. That was crazy!"

I help her out of our car, and then we nod and smile at the bride and groom, and start looking for... well, shit. Who are we looking for?

"What do we do now?" Emma asks.

"I dunno. Grandma left."

"Maybe Clarence is waiting for us back inside the hotel?"

We follow the wedding party down the walkway

that leads back into the hotel, and then pause below the Big Apple Coaster sign to look around.

"I don't see him," Emma says.

I don't either. I pull out my phone to check the time, just to make sure we're still on schedule—we are. It's only ten minutes to ten—and then a text pops up.

Meet Larry in front of the reception desk downstairs.

I hold up the phone for Emma so she can see the message. "I guess we go downstairs."

Larry ends up being a short, pot-bellied Hispanic dude with a thick, black mustache wearing a blue velour track suit with a white stripe going up the middle of his body. He rushes us as we look around. "Jesse and Emma," he says in a thick Spanish accent. "Follow me. We're off to Treasure Island for a pirate wedding!"

Emma squeezes my hand. "That sounds fun!"

"We have to run," Larry says. "It's about to start. Let's go."

"Run?" Emma asks. But Larry is jogging towards the lobby entrance.

"Come on," I say, taking off and dragging her behind me. "Pirate wedding totally sounds fun. And we're in a hurry anyway, right?"

We have one hour before we need to be back at the airport and on our way to Florida.

CHAPTER TWELVE

OK, I get it. What we're doing here in Vegas is the definition of budget wedding. But would it kill them to drive us over to Treasure Island in the Fingermobile? And/or give us the option of grabbing a cab? Because even though at one point on that coaster I could *see* Treasure Island down the Strip, it's not *at all* close to New York, New York. Like over a mile. So by the time we skid into the lobby I have a cramp in my side and I feel like I'm about to die.

"No one said there was an athletic requirement!" I complain to Jesse as I bend over and try to breathe. He's out of breath too, and we're both slick with sweat even though it's not even that hot out. You run a mile down the Las Vegas Strip and you're a sticky mess when you arrive at your destination no matter what.

"This way," Larry snaps.

"Come on," Jesse says. "We only have forty-five minutes for two weddings. We have to make this quick!"

And even though everything does go very fast for the next five minutes—we make our way down a hallway and into the staging area for the Treasure Island pirate show—everything comes to a screeching halt once we arrive.

Again, there is already another wedding planned. And again, there is a bundle of money involved as Larry talks to the bride and groom.

But this time, they do not take the money. They stand firm. No way. No how. They are not gonna do it.

But Larry is cool and calm. He pulls out yet another bundle of money from a hidden pocket inside his blue velour track jacket.

Jesse says, "Shit. Do you think those are fifties? Or hundreds?"

I have no idea. But it doesn't matter. The bride and groom hold firm and shake their heads again.

Larry approaches, frowning. "They want more because they had the deluxe package with a top-notch photographer and there's no way to fit them in the schedule for later today. It's full."

"More than what?" Jesse asks. "Not that I care."

He looks at me with a smile. "I'm OK with paying them if we can get this moving. But… how much are we talking here?"

"I offered them twenty."

"Twenty thousand dollars?" I ask.

"They said no."

"OK. Double it," Jesse says. "Give them forty."

I look down at myself. I'm just wearing jeans and a t-shirt. And that's fine, I guess. But I'm so hot and my hair is a mess. "If we get a professional photographer, I can't get married in this! I'm all sweaty and gross from running down the Strip!" I shoot Larry a glare at that last part. Because what the fuck? Why have a Fingermobile if you're not going to use it?

"I can ask if they will throw in the dress," Larry offers. "But it might cost you another ten grand."

I eyeball the bride's dress. She looks like she stepped straight out of a heavy metal music video from nineteen eighty-eight. I'm talking a white high-low leather dress with a ragged sharkbite hem and shoulder pads with spiky metal studs lining the long sleeves of her arms. But the best part—ha—is the white leather thigh-high boots with matching metal spikes and the white-lace fingerless gloves. The groom looks like he might actually work somewhere nearby as a Bon Jovi lookalike.

They seem to be taking this whole pirate wedding thing very literally.

"No way," I tell Jesse. "I'm not wearing that."

Jesse sighs and runs his fingers through his hair. He pulls out his phone and checks the time. "Babe. We only have thirty minutes before we have to leave. We're not gonna make it to the third wedding at this point."

"But my custom dress! The mean Russian lady is working so hard on it!"

"I know. But…" He looks at the bride and groom, then back at me. "This might be our only chance to have a real wedding."

"My hair is a mess too," I whine. "I don't want wedding photos of me looking like some metal-head wannabe!"

"OK, hold on," Larry says. "I have an idea." He holds up one finger and then walks off to the bride and groom.

"Oh, fuck. He just pulled out three more straps of money," Jesse says. He looks at me again. "I'm not complaining about the money, OK—"

"I don't care about the money." But that certainly explains his pot belly under the track suit. It was literally made of money. "If we have to leave in thirty minutes, fine. But that wedding on the coaster was… I mean, what was that?"

"I don't know. It was weird, right?"

"It definitely wasn't legal. I did scream 'I do,' but I'm not Karen and you're not Chad."

"Do we even have the legal paperwork to get married?"

"No clue."

"I'm starting to have serious doubts about Fingers' Fantasy Weddings."

"Starting?" I laugh.

"I knew this was a scam. Maybe we should just skip it and go home?"

I'm actually considering that when Larry comes back. "OK. We've got it all sorted. They took the fifty grand and the dress—"

"I'm not wearing that dress."

"No," Larry agrees. "They said it's custom and cost well over what I just paid for the bribe—"

I snort. Whatever.

"—but the costume department said they will dress you for the wedding for an extra one large."

I look at Jesse and he shrugs. "What's a thousand dollars more at this point, right?"

I nod and actually smile. "A real pirate wedding?" I ask Larry.

"Real pirate wedding. All the actors are ready for this one. They even have a wig for you, Miss Emma."

I clap. "OK. Let's do this!"

Immediately a team of people appear and whisk me down a hallway. I look over my shoulder at Jesse, but he's being whisked away by another team in the opposite direction. And I don't know... this kinda maybe feels more like how it's supposed to be. Both of us getting ready in different places so we'll be surprised when we meet up again.

And all this is going to happen on a pirate ship!

My team directs me to a makeup chair in front of a mirror and gets busy. Two girls are putting make-up on me at once. Like... lots of makeup. Stage makeup, I realize. But OK. I get it. It's a show. Plus, they do this every day. They must know what looks good.

Then a selection of wigs is brought out. All of them are very... *pirate wench*. But that's fun, right? I choose a long red one with lots of waves. But wigs aren't something I'm used to, so I'm surprised when they pull my hair back into a skull cap to get it all tucked away.

And the makeup is going on a little bit heavy... like my eyes are not smoky, they're practically pits of darkness. Still, when the wig goes on for styling, it looks good. I don't look like Emma anymore. But it's fun.

I keep telling myself that as my wardrobe choices are presented. There's a skimpy siren option—no, thank you. A long, ruffly thing that looks like a Victorian dressing gown. Pass. And a vintage white, off-the-shoulder mini-dress with a long lace train. It has more ruffles than I'm comfortable with, and the bell sleeves are way too wide to be practical, but it's the only one that looks a little bit like a wedding dress. So I choose that.

It comes with knee-high boots that lace all the way up and it takes two people to get them on me. But ten minutes later they pull me out of the chair and twirl me in front of a full-length mirror.

Not bad… if you look at me from far away like the spectators who watch the pirate show.

But Jesse isn't going to be looking at me from far away. This is a close-up moment if ever there was one. And I look like… Emma Dumas playing dress-up for a Vegas pirate show.

I cringe. Do I really want my wedding memories to be of wigs and gaudy make-up, a pirate mini-dress that looks more like a Halloween costume than a wedding dress, and knee-high boots?

No. No, I don't. But not many people can say they got married on a pirate ship, right?

Then I rally. Because at least this is *my* decision. My mother would die—like *die*—if she were here. She would drag me away, call me insane, and then boss me back to Key West, pronto.

So I nod my head and smile at the team. "It's perfect. I'm ready. Take me to my buccaneer groom!"

Maybe it's not the dream wedding, but that's how all perfectly planned moments go, right? They never turn out the way you think. There's always a reality check.

Besides, we're out of time. We need to be back home for Christmas Eve dinner or my mother will *kill* me. The whole 'till death do us part' thing will happen a lot sooner than we think if we don't make it back in time for her carefully planned festivities.

They whisk me out of the room, down the hall, and I just get a glimpse of Jesse in full-on swashbuckling pirate gear as I'm led up a set of stairs and he's pulled in the opposite direction.

Suddenly I'm surrounded by a bunch of scantily-clad women who are obviously part of the show.

"Just follow our lead," one of them says.

"It'll be OK, don't be afraid," another whispers in my ear.

"And when they set you free, just go with it. I promise you won't fall," the first adds.

"Wait." I blink my eyes. "What?" But before I can ask responsible, pertinent questions about what the fuck 'I promise you won't fall' means, I'm pushed through a curtain and walked out—

"Ho-lee shit," I breathe.

I'm on the top level of the pirate ship looking down on a thousand people surrounding the front of the hotel, waiting for the show to start.

I turn to the girl next to me, a bouncy blonde wearing a fluffy pink and green tutu skirt. "What's happening?"

And that's when the music starts and flames start shooting up the wall behind me.

I jump. Because hot damn. That geyser of fire puts out some heat!

Then all the girls are dancing and swaying to the beat of the music. One pushes me forward and I stumble out onto a platform, then make the mistake of looking down.

"Shit!" I squeal, taking two steps back. But they push me forward again, and then two of them are lifting my hands up in the air and clamping thick metal bracelets onto my wrists. "Wait!" I yell.

But they do not wait. They attach my new bracelets to a chain affixed to the ship's mast.

The show must go on, I guess.

I'm up in the crow's nest, I realize. I scan the deck down below, looking for Jesse, but all I see are the siren girls, dancing around and having a good time.

Then a horn blasts, and more flames are shooting out across the little bridge. Another pirate ship. And that's where all the buccaneers are.

I get lost in that sight for a moment. Because there's like three dozen dancing, shirtless men over there and they are pret-*ty* nice to look at.

Suddenly a sword fight breaks out and then there's mass commotion, and the next thing I know, bare-chested muscly pirates are flying towards me on ropes.

"Emma!" one of them yells.

I laugh hysterically when I realize it's Jesse. All dressed up in a puffy shirt and baggy pants with pirate boots on.

He swings towards me with wide, surprised eyes—then goes right past as all the other men jump off their ropes and land in the rigging around the mast and sail.

I try to turn to see where Jesse is, but I don't have to look hard, because he comes swaying back my way, still yelling, "Emma!"

One of the more experienced actors grabs his rope as it goes by and for a moment, I'm positive the sudden jerk will shake Jesse off the rope. But he holds tight. Clings to it, actually. And then two guys are pulling him off the swinging rope and onto the rigging. He shimmies up towards me and I know I should be worried about him falling two stories down onto that deck below, but all I can think about is—no one asked me if I knew how to climb a rope!

I don't.

I suck at rope climbing.

But luckily, Jesse is a sailor, and he's got this. And I'm just going to assume there's no rope climbing in my future, because that would not end well and anyway, there's no time to think about that. Because six hot pirates are all dancing around me now like this is the Magic Mike show.

I laugh.

Best wedding ever!

One leans into my ear and whispers, "Hey there, Emma. Don't worry. We won't let you fall. But you better hold onto me tight!"

"Ooo-kay," I stammer. But then I'm like, "Wait. Should I be worried about—"

Before I can finish my sentence, they've freed me from my siren cuffs, and one of them grabs me by the waist.

I see Jesse climbing up the rigging, and he finally gets to the crow's nest when the freaking pirate I'm now attached to jumps off.

We go sailing through the air.

I scream, "Holy *fuuuuuuuuuck*!"

Jesse yells, "Emmaaaaaaaa!"

Then we land precariously on the rigging and another pirate is there, whisking me into his arms. And before I even have a chance to appreciate his hot, sweaty, muscly body, we jump again.

This time we slide down the rope and I'm sure— like one hundred percent for sure—we're going to die. But just before we crash into the deck, the fall slows to a stop and when I look up, I see that the pirate holding onto me was using a rope-brake to slow us down.

My heart is galloping with adrenaline inside my chest. I place my hand over it, trying to focus on the show going on around me and figure out where Jesse is now.

It's fake. It's all fake, Emma.

I know this, but there's so much happening my heart is having a hard time believing that.

"Emmaaaaaaaa!"

I turn to see Jesse swinging towards me on a rope. His shirt is flapping open and I get a good long look at his beautiful chest. "Jesseeeeeee!" I yell back.

His foot actually touches the rigging just above my head, but then another pirate is there, pulling Jesse off. They crash to the deck. Luckily it's only about six feet and Jesse lands on top of the enemy pirate, and then he's up on his feet, drawing his sword.

Oh. I get it. He's the good pirate sent to save me,

the damsel in distress.

The other pirate draws his sword too and then there's a flurry of clashing and twirling.

I'm pulled away—I think this is for my safety—but then… "HOL-LEEEE SHIT!"

A whole group of them lift me up in the air and start running.

I don't know what else to do at this point but laugh. "Jesseeeeee," I yell, turning around on my stomach with my arms extended, reaching for him.

He smiles at me, then with one whoosh of his sword, he connects with the enemy sword and that guy falls down to the deck and starts acting out a whole fake death scene.

Meanwhile, I'm set back down on my feet in front of the plank.

They're not serious, right? I laugh at them.

But then one of them starts dragging me out over the water. This is when I notice the crowd again. Because they go wild and start chanting things like, "Throw her over!" and "Jump! Jump! Jump!"

I look down at the water beneath me, struggling to stay as close to the ship's deck as I possibly can.

It kinda feels real. Like this bushy-beard head pirate guy really might throw me over.

"No," I say, shaking my head at him. "Nope. I'm

not jumping! I'm getting married!"

He just grins at me. And… is that a gold tooth?

Suddenly a parrot attacks him, landing on his head and flapping wildly. I squeal. The crowd cheers, on my side again.

Then Jesse is here, pulling me back onto the ship's deck and wrapping his arms around me. "Emma," he says, pulling me into a tight hug.

I look up at him and smile. "Best wedding ever!"

Then a whole bunch of flames start shooting up behind the ship and the battle is on! We just stand and watch the rest of the show, every now and then scrambling out of the way of the performers as they sing and dance.

But then… then we're being pulled up a flight of stairs and everyone is waving goodbye.

"Wait!" I yell to Jesse. "We didn't get married yet!"

"Hey!" Jesse yells. But we're tugged and pulled backstage and then everyone is high-fiving and shouting excitedly.

"Hey," Jesse yells again. "What about the wedding?"

"Oh," one of the head pirates says. "That happens in the chapel."

"But…" I look back at the stage door that leads outside. "The ship!"

"Sorry," one of the sirens says. "No weddings on the ship."

"Then what was this whole show?" Jesse asks. "And the couple who were here before?"

"Oh, that was Jake and Cynthia," the pirate says. "They work here."

"What?" Jesse and I both exclaim.

"Yeah," the siren says. "This is the Save the Beauty Show. They're the stars." She shakes her head. "I don't know how much you paid to take their places, but that was the most fun I've had doing this show in years. Congrats!"

And then everyone is walking off.

I look at Jesse and pout. "We're not even married!"

He looks down at his watch. "Shit. And it's eleven twenty! We're late." He pats his pants, looking for his phone. "Shit."

"Do not tell me you dropped your phone during the sword fight!"

"I did. It's not here. I don't even have my wallet. I knew these pants were too baggy. Where's yours?"

"In my purse"—I whirl around, looking for the way back to the dressing room I was in—"back in the dressing room."

"Let's go find it. Maybe the crew is still waiting for us. We can call them and let them know we're on our way."

"But we're not even married!"

He takes my hand and tugs me along, in search of the dressing rooms. "Maybe the captain can marry us on the flight back? That's a thing, right?"

"Maybe? I don't know. But we cannot go back to Key West until we're married! That defeats the whole purpose of the trip."

"We'll figure it out. But we have to go. Now! We're going to miss Christmas Eve dinner!"

CHAPTER THIRTEEN

When we finally find the dressing rooms again, Emma's purse is gone and the clock on the wall says it's now eleven thirty-seven.

There's no sign of Steve, or Clarence, or Fingers—anywhere.

Emma is pouting about the purse, and the wedding—or lack thereof—and telling me her boots are too small and she can't run. So I help her wobble her way down to the front desk of the hotel and I'm just about to ask the concierge if I can use their phone to call—someone. I don't even have the number for the fucking charter service because Miles set that up and all the info was in my little black folder—also now missing—when a woman steps in front of us.

"Emma and Jesse?" she asks.

"Yes?" I say. She's tall, thin, and wearing a dark

blue pantsuit with a name tag that says, 'Fingers' Fantasy Weddings. Hello, my name is Jessica.' I stop and say, "Oh, thank God! We need to get to the airport right now!"

"I hope you brought the Fingermobile," Emma says. "Because I refuse to run to the airport in these boots!"

"I'm on it," Jessica says. "Follow me. And yes, Miss Dumas. We have the van ready to take you to the airport."

"Whew," I say, glancing at Emma. "We're gonna make it. And don't worry. We will be married before we get home, babe. I promise!"

Everyone is staring at us when we walk out to the valet area and head towards the purple van. And then I realize we're still wearing our pirate clothes. I feel more than a little ridiculous in my puffy shirt, but fuck it. Two seconds later we're climbing into the back of the van and the crazy world of Treasure Island disappears when Jessica slides the door shut.

I lean back in the couch, still holding Emma's hand. Then we look at each other and laugh.

"Did that really just happen?" She giggles.

"I think it did. I'm not sure. I was so confused, I barely remember anything."

"I remember your face when you were swinging

towards me on that rope and then went sailing by."

I laugh. Loudly. "I thought I was gonna die like six times!"

"Only six?"

"Seriously, that *was* fun though, right?"

"Pretty fuckin' fun, Mr. Boston! Except—"

"I know." I bring her hand up to my lips and kiss it. "We're not married yet. But I'm pretty sure the pilot can marry us on the plane. I really do think that's a thing."

"I hope so. Even if we didn't get married for real on the rollercoaster or the pirate ship, it was a pretty fun morning."

It actually was.

"I'm sad that we're going to miss the last wedding though. I think that was the real one that counts. And I wanted the dress."

"And the cake," I add. "I'm so hungry right now."

"I think you just burned like two thousand calories swinging on those ropes."

We laugh and she sinks into me. I put my arm around her and decide, if this turns out to be the highlight of our wedding day, it's still pretty up there as far as cool times go.

It takes forever to get over to the airport, even though it's only a few miles away. And by the time the van stops next to the charter drop I have a feeling it's after noon.

"Your mom is gonna be pissed at us," I say.

"I know. If it's like… noon, and we take off at twelve thirty, with the time change we won't land until well after eight o'clock."

"We'll call them from the plane and tell them we'll be late."

"Yeah. OK. I mean, what else can we do? We're more than two thousand miles away from home."

Which is crazy. But that's pretty much the story of my life.

The van door slides open and Jessica is there. "OK, kids. We're here. Follow Sven there and he'll get you all set up."

I furrow my brows as we climb out of the van. "Set up for what?"

"Your third wedding. Parachuting!"

"What?" Emma says.

"No," I say. "We have to leave now. We have a charter jet—" I look around, trying to figure out where the jet might be. "Well, it's somewhere around here."

"Oh," Jessica says. "I'm so sorry. I didn't realize. I thought you understood when you said we needed to get to the airport."

"Yeah, for our charter jet." I'm still trying to find

it, but the only thing I see are a bunch of helicopters and one plane that says 'Sven's Skydiving.' "Do you have a phone I can borrow?"

"Sure," Jessica says. She fishes it out of her pocket and hands it over.

I look at Emma. "You don't happen to know Miles' phone number off hand, do you?"

"Uh… no."

"Shit. What should we do?"

"How about," Jessica offers, taking her phone back, "you two go inside the office and I'll figure out where your charter is?"

"Yeah," I say, running my fingers through my hair. "OK. Yes." I turn to Emma. "We could use a few moments of quiet contemplation right about now. It's been a crazy morning."

"Good. It's right through there." She points to a metal door with no window. "I'll check on your charter and be right back."

"OK." Emma sighs. We walk towards the door, go inside, and practically run into a huge blond dude, who surely must be Sven.

"Ah, there you are!" he says in a booming voice. Then he slaps me on the back so hard, I almost choke. "Or should I say, 'Arrgggggh, mateys!'"

"Funny." Emma chuckles.

"Seriously," Sven says, his face going somber. "We're running late, folks. So we have to hustle."

"We're not doing it," I tell him.

"What?"

"Yeah, we have to go," Emma says. "Our charter jet is waiting to take us back to Key West. We just need to figure out where it is."

Sven frowns at me. "But this is your big moment. Don't you two want to get married?"

"We do," I say. "We're just out of time. We're already gonna miss Christmas Eve dinner."

"Well, if you're already late…?" Sven pans his arms wide. Like… *Might as well be really late.*

Emma and I look at each other. It's one of those should-we-shouldn't-we? looks.

She shrugs. "We *have* to be married when we land. And at this point we don't even know if we have a charter."

"True," I say. "So…" I glance at the skydiving pictures all around me. "Wanna jump out of a plane with me?"

"I do," she squeals.

"Perfect," Sven booms. "OK. Let's get you out of those pirate clothes and into some jumpsuits."

"Wait," Emma says. "What about my dress?"

Sven makes one of those looks. Not one that says

should-we-shouldn't-we, but one that says, *Fuck. Fuck, fuck, fuck.* "I'm afraid… the dress isn't ready yet."

"Nooooo," Emma pouts. "I *need* the dress."

Sven shrugs. "Sorry. But don't worry. Fingers will make it right when the final bill comes in."

And that has me wondering… I wonder what that final bill will look like? We've got to be pushing a hundred grand at this point. After that Treasure Island bribe? Yeah. This is a pretty pricey wedding day and we're not even married yet.

I turn to Emma. "I know you're disappointed, but we could be stuck here. We're clearly not going to make it home in time for dinner. So we should just… do this, right?"

She sighs, heavily.

"I'll make it up to you, Emma. I promise. We'll have the mean Russian lady ship your dress and we'll have another ridiculous wedding anywhere you want."

She leans into me. "OK." Then she tilts her head up and her eyes catch mine. "I love you."

"God, I love you too." I place my hand on her cheek as I lean down to kiss her lips. "The thought of jumping out of a plane kinda terrifies me. But not because I'm afraid I'll get hurt or die." I look up at Sven. "This is safe, right? Because if my wife gets hurt, I will not let that go."

"Very safe, Mr. Boston. I promise you. We have completed over five hundred tandem jumps over the past ten years with a perfect safety record. We will be with you the entire time and you'll each have a headset to hear the captain of the plane as he recites the marriage rites."

I point at Emma. "I knew captains could marry people."

"Follow me and we'll get you situated in your jumpsuits and gear."

Once we change out of our pirate clothes and put on our jumpsuits, the crew goes over the tandem harness we'll be strapped into. It would be better if Emma and I could be together for the jump, but apparently there's rules about that and you have to take some kind of training course if you want to jump alone.

But the crew have assured us that they will maneuver us close enough to briefly hold hands and if we get the timing right, we can do that in the moment we say 'I do.' Then we'll drift apart, the chutes will be released, and we'll be back on the ground in about twenty seconds.

And actually, if you add up the whole thing from start to finish, we should be done by one thirty and if

Jessica can find our charter, we could be back in Key West to open presents at midnight.

Not a bad way to spend twenty-four hours of your life.

Or your wedding day, for that matter.

Once we're in the plane, Sven gives us our helmet headsets and does a mic check to make sure we can all hear each other. We can. Sounds pretty crisp and clear, if you ask me. And even though skydiving would've been my last choice off the crazy Vegas wedding menu, I'm pretty excited about it.

Emma and I buckle into our jump seats near the door of the plane and hold hands. "Are you nervous?" I ask.

She sucks in a deep breath and nods. "I am. But it's the good kind of nervous. Not wedding-day jitters."

"Ha. We've been through this twice now. One more and we'll overtake Miles in the wedding department."

"Speaking of Miles, there has to be a way to contact him."

"Well, there's the map."

"The crazy poker game map?" She rolls her eyes.

"I'm telling you, Emma. He told me a whole story about how he grew up in the Mob."

"A story. That's all it was."

"Why would he lie to me about that? It makes no sense. And Fingers? This whole day was his idea."

"I don't know, but we did a thorough background check on him before I hired him."

"I'm sure you did a thorough background check on me at one point too, right?"

"Not the point."

"Totally the point! Anyway. I kinda remember the map. After this we can go see if we can find him. He'll know what to do."

"Everyone ready?" Sven asks, pulling on our harnesses to make sure we're secure.

I'm not really sure I'm ready for this, but here we are. And if this is our only shot at a wedding today, it is what it is.

"Ready." Emma answers for both of us.

Sven goes over the procedure as the plane begins to taxi. We're gonna go up to cruising altitude, which is just about fourteen thousand feet. Then, as the plane gets into position, Emma and I will be clipped to the harness of Sven and his buddy, Blain. The ceremony starts in the helmet headsets, we all jump out, link up on the way down, hold hands for a few seconds, say "I do," drop hands, parachutes release, land on the ground—presto. We're married.

Who knew getting married in Vegas could be so hard? Hopefully third time's a charm.

I look over at Emma, take her hand, and smile. "This is it, babe. It's really gonna happen this time. For real. Nothing can go wrong."

"Jesse. We're in a plane and in ten minutes we're going to jump out of it. *Everything* can go wrong."

"Yeah, but… I was only talking about the wedding."

She laughs and shakes her head. Then the plane takes off and we're slammed into the hard backs of our jump seats. My heart starts to beat fast, but not so much because we're about to skydive. We really are going to get married this time. This is it. Our moment when we pledge our love to each other forever.

As the plane climbs up into the sky I think back on those first few moments when we met back in Mallory Square. I never forgot her. OK, maybe I forgot her a little bit since I didn't immediately recognize her when she was kidnapping me that night of the bachelor auction, but this girl has been in the back of my mind for over a decade. I always knew there was something wrong with me. Something missing. I just couldn't put my finger on what it was until Emma took me on a dream date.

Now it feels like we were never apart. I know that's dumb since we were apart for thirteen years, but we just slid right into this new relationship like we didn't miss a single minute. We really are 'that couple' and this whole adventure in Vegas just proves it. Because for sure, it's been a crazy few hours, but I kinda love this craziness almost as much as I love Emma Dumas.

Sven's voice is suddenly in my head. "OK, folks. This is it. Let's get hitched!"

Sven unbuckles me and Blain unbuckles Emma. And then we're standing up and they're clipping us to the tandem harnesses. Just as that happens, another guy whooshes open the door of the plane and the wind whips in.

The captain's voice is now in our helmets as Sven and Blain maneuver us towards the edge.

"We are gathered here together today to join Emma and Jesse as…" the captain begins.

"Holy shit," Emma says. "What are we doing?"

"It's OK," Blain assures her with a little nudge towards the open door.

"… they proclaim their love and commitment to the world. This is a moment for reflection, and rejoicing. To acknowledge their bond and…"

"OK, let's go, folks!" Sven yells over the captain's

speech.

And then I'm thinking… *Yeah, what the hell are we doing? We're gonna jump out of a plane?* "Wait!"

But it's too late. Sven pushes me forward and we go tumbling out the door. And even with the helmet on, the whipping wind is loud. My suit is flapping and it's cold. Very cold.

"Holy shit!" I yell.

Over the headset, the captain continues. "Jesse, you are here to proclaim your love for Emma. Emma, you are here to pledge yourself to Jesse…"

Then… there she is. Emma. My beautiful bride. Laughing and smiling as she reaches for me with her hands. And somehow, Sven and Blain have maneuvered us so we're facing each other. I reach for her too. Our fingertips touch and I grab onto her with everything I can and pull her closer to me.

"Do you, Jesse…" But that's all I hear. Or, actually, I hear things, but only static.

"Hey!" I yell. "I can't hear!" But my voice sounds muffled and distant. "My headset stopped working! I can't hear the vows!"

Emma's saying something too. Then her hand slips out from mine and she floats away.

"Emmaaaa!"

I see her say, "Jesseeeee!" And then…

Whoosh!

She flies upwards and disappears from my view.

What the fuck? We didn't even say 'I do!'

But then I'm jerked upwards and holy fuck. The harness cuts into the soft flesh under my arms and it fuckin' hurts.

But there's no time to think about that because the earth is getting closer and closer. Sven maneuvers us in small circles, and then before I know it our feet are on the ground and we're running.

Of course, I trip, fall down, and take Sven with me.

He unclips us, turns me over, and holds out his hand.

I take it and let him pull me to my feet. But as soon as I'm steady, I take off my helmet. "What the hell was that?"

He claps me on the back. Pretty hard. Too hard, actually. "Congratulations!"

"Congratulations? We didn't even say 'I do!'"

"What?"

"Dude." I point to him. "Do not fuck with me. You know we didn't say 'I do' because the headsets stopped working just as we got to the vows."

"Awww. Nah. That's not what happened. I heard you say 'I do.'"

"I did not say 'I do.'" I look around and find Emma

coming towards me, pulling off her helmet and shaking out her hair. She's smiling big.

"Oh. My. God!" she says, nearly breathless. "That was the best wedding ever!"

"What? No! I couldn't hear! I didn't say 'I do!'"

Emma frowns. "What? Are you sure? I thought I heard you say—"

"I didn't! I couldn't hear anything after 'Do you, Jesse!'"

"Oh. Well…" She looks at Sven. "Well, that sucks."

"It's still legal," Sven insists.

"How can it be legal?" I ask. "And that's not even the point! I didn't get to say 'I do!'"

"Maybe we can do it again?" Emma offers.

But both Sven and Blain are both shaking their heads. "No can do," Sven says.

"We're booked up for the rest of the day," Blain adds.

I turn away and take a deep breath. Because you know what? Fuck this.

"Fuck this," I say. "We're out of here. I'm so done with weddings. Fingers can just fuck off. His fantasy weddings were all bullshit and fake. That Treasure Island wedding? Not even a wedding! He lied to us and we actually took the place of the freaking show performers! And that Big Apple Coaster wedding? We weren't even the couple getting married! This whole thing is a scam!"

I take Emma's hand and tug her along after me as we head back towards the hangar where our clothes are.

And fuck me now. All we have to wear is pirate clothes.

I want to kill someone. Mostly someone called Fingers.

Emma lets me lead her back into the hangar office without comment. But once we're inside and I finally look at her, she's pouting.

"I'm sorry," I say. "I'm sorry. It's been a great day. It really has. But…"

"But we wanted to get married. That was the whole point. And if you didn't get to say 'I do,' then we didn't really accomplish that, did we?"

"No," I say, feeling defeated. "And where the hell is Jessica? Wasn't she supposed to go find our charter? We should just go home."

Emma looks around. "She never came back, I guess."

"Big surprise there. So far we've been handed off after each fuckup. I wonder who will pop up now?"

"Maybe no one," Emma says, pulling off her

jumpsuit.

I take mine off too, and then reluctantly put my pirate clothes back on.

Emma is in the middle of doing the same with her dress when she points to me and snaps her fingers. "You know what?"

"What?"

"Who cares about the charter? We have a jet here. Right here!" She points to the ground. "Somewhere, in one of these hangars, is my Bright Berry Beach jet."

For a moment I allow myself to get lost in the thought of finding that jet. I get lost in the idea of changing into new clothes—surely Miles comes prepared with clothes? And if not, there has to be some silk pajamas hidden somewhere on board. Beats the hell out of pirate pants and puffy shirts.

"But we can't go home. Not without Christopher. And I'm sure he and Miles are busy with the poker tournament by now."

"I don't even care if we go home," Emma says. "I just want to climb aboard my jet and relax. I'm freaking exhausted!"

"Me too."

"Let's just find it and wait for Christopher and Miles to come back."

"We're gonna miss Christmas, Emma."

She shrugs. "I don't care. I mean, I do care. That totally sucks because I had the best present for you. But I literally have no fucks left to give today. I'm ready for a nap. Let's find the jet and take a nap." Then she waggles her eyebrows at me.

"Ahhh," I say, my spirits lifting. "A nap."

She giggles. "I know this whole day has been one disaster after another, but it was still fun, right? Even if we're not even married yet." Then her whole face goes serious. "You know what? I would not put it past my mother to call up Fingers and boss him into ruining all our weddings just so she could get her way. In fact, I bet that stupid Kraken Karen went right over to my parents' house after we ditched her and told her that we stole her Door Dash."

"That's ridiculous."

"Is it? Is it, really? You've seen my mother in action. She's an unstoppable force. I would not put it past her to somehow figure out we eloped to Vegas and then boss everyone in the family into fucking it all up."

"Emma," I say, trying not to laugh. "That's crazy. None of this is about your mother. It's all... *Miles.*"

She sucks in a deep breath. "For the last time, Miles is *not* Mob!"

"Fine, fine." I put up my hands in surrender. "If

you say so. But I'm really on board with just finding the jet and staying put until we can get a hold of Miles. That's a solid plan if you ask me."

"Good. I don't think I could handle another wedding."

"We're all out of weddings, babe. Our Pick Three is done."

We finish getting dressed and we're just about to walk back out into Sven's office when I point to the bathroom. "You might want to check your makeup, Ems. The wind kinda messed it up."

"Oh, fuck it. I don't care. It can wait until we get to the jet."

As soon as we exit the dressing room Sven is on his feet with hands in the air. "I'm really sorry about the glitch up in the air. We'd like to make it up to you. No charge for this package. It's on us. I've already called up Fingers and told him about the mix-up. He's sending Vinnie over right now to make things right and get you another wedding set up pronto."

"Forget it," I say. "We're done. We've got our own jet somewhere in this airport. We're heading over there to wait for our pilot to show up."

"But... Vinnie!" Sven calls after us.

We ignore him.

I hold the office door open for Emma and we

saunter out to go find the Bright Berry Beach jet.

It takes a good while to find our way over to the charter area where they schedule flights in and out for private jets. And even though I know damn well that Jessica chick never came over here to find our charter, I keep my eyes peeled for her anyway. I'm really not in the mood to deal with the minions of Fingers. I just want to board Emma's plane, relax in a soft leather chair, take a nap in the jet bedroom, and hopefully fuck my future wife.

But here's the thing. When you walk into a jet club wearing pirate outfits, they tend to not take you seriously.

"I swear to God, I am Emma Dumas."

The check-in woman eyeballs my almost-wife with suspicion. Pirate clothes aside, everything about us right now screams chaos. And she is having none of it.

"I'm sorry, ma'am. I'm going to need some form of ID." Her Southern accent sounds sweet, but it's laced with disbelief.

"We lost our IDs at the Treasure Island pirate show. Why the hell else would we be dressed like pirates if we weren't in the freaking show?"

"Ma'am, I understand what you're saying. But people dress like pirates for all sorts of reasons. And regardless of what they are, we still require ID to gain access to the jets."

"It's *my* jet. I'm Emma Dumas. I'm one-fourth owner of Bright Berry Beach cosmetics. The freaking plane is black with 'Bright Berry Beach' written across the fuselage in screaming pink letters! It's. *My*. Jet!"

"And yet," the skeptical woman says, "you cannot prove that."

"Just look me up online! And this"—Emma pushes me in front of her—"this is Jesse Boston! All you have to do is one internet search and you'll see we're telling the truth! Now search us!"

The woman blinks at Emma, then presses her lips together and begins typing on her computer. She looks at the screen. Then us. Then the screen again. Then us.

"Well?" Emma is out of patience.

"I see some resemblance."

"Some—" Emma takes a deep breath. "Are you, or are you not, going to tell me where my freaking jet is located?"

"Fine. It's in hangar seventeen C. But it's not scheduled to fly out today, so there's two other jets in front of it at the moment so—"

"We're not leaving. We just want to go on board

and wait for our butler to finish his poker game."

"Then there you go. Hangar seventeen is right out those doors and to the left." She flips her hand off towards the door.

"Thank you!" Emma exclaims. Then she sucks in a deep breath, takes my hand, and says, "Let's go."

I wait until we're outside before I say, "God. I love it when you're bossy."

She shakes her head and huffs out a laugh. "Jesus Christ. This day is… just…"

"Yeah," I agree. We need some jet time for sure.

Hangar seventeen isn't just outside and to the left though. I mean, technically it is. But we have to weave our way through parked jets and other hangars before we finally find it almost a quarter mile away.

And that's when we realize mistake number one.

"Hmm…" Emma is tapping her chin with her forefinger. "How do you open the door?"

I throw up my hands and walk over to the front wheel, then precariously take a seat on top of the tire. "No fuckin' clue, babe."

She turns to me. "We did not come this far to be locked out of our own jet."

"Didn't we though?" I laugh. I can't help it.

"Surely there's a way to open the door and pull down the stairs?"

I shrug. "Your guess is as good as mine."

"Look. It can't be that hard. This is the handle, right?"

"I'm pretty sure it's locked. I'm also pretty sure Miles is the one with the key."

"But maybe… see? There's this little button. I think I've seen Miles open the door with this button." She presses the button.

Nothing happens.

"OK, so maybe there's a trick with the handle and the button?"

I sigh. I'm actually kinda sore from all that rope-swinging and sword-fighting. But I get up and walk over to it because I really do want to just go inside and collapse. I study the side of the plane, trying to work out the meaning of the button and the handle.

Then I glance over at the jet in front of ours and notice there's some writing on the door. And sure enough, when I walk over to it, there are instructions. Instructions which have been conveniently left off of Emma's jet because it's got that fancy custom black paint job.

"Hold the button and turn the handle at the same time," I call to Emma.

She does that and then squeals with delight. "We did it!"

"Thank God."

She slowly lowers the small set of airstairs and we use the last of our energy to climb them and enter the front cabin.

Then we look at each other and realize mistake number two.

"We don't have power," she says. Because the engines aren't on.

I just laugh. Fuck it. I take her hand, drag her back to the bedroom, and we collapse onto the mattress.

I don't even care about power. At least we now have a home base away from the crazy world of Fingers' Fantasy Vegas Weddings. And even though I would really like to tackle my almost-bride and take all her clothes off, the next thing I know she's blissfully asleep.

CHAPTER FOURTEEN

I'm in the middle of the most delicious dream.

My wedding, the way I imagined it. Not this crazy Vegas adventure. Not my mother's Krakken version of the big day. Mine. All mine.

In this version of Emma and Jesse's Christmas Eve Wedding Fantasy everything is dreamy and surreal and no one is stressed or disappointed and nothing goes wrong.

All our family members are there. My parents, my brothers—hell, even my childhood dog is there. And Jesse's brothers and almost-sister-and-brother-in-laws.

The dress is amazing. A tight, form-fitting mermaid dress that hugs all my curves and makes Jesse look at me hungrily. He's dressed up like a billionaire bad boy in a black tux, his hair just a little bit disheveled, just enough to look sexy but not unkempt.

207

And his smile—God, his smile as I make my way towards him is something worth memorizing. Something to be treasured. Something I wish I could capture in a bottle and save for a dark day.

I have a long train being held up by little flower-girl Maisy as I walk down the aisle and my dad is beaming at me as he guides me up the steps and hands me off to Jesse at the altar.

My stomach is filled with happy jitters. My heart is beating fast, but it's not a *thump-thump*, *thump-thump*, like the sound effects in a horror movie. It's like the hoofbeats of a galloping horse on the beach where the surf meets the sand. A powerful but soft beat. A strong but smooth rhythm.

My father kisses me on the cheek as Jesse takes my hand, his eyes locked on mine like there is no one else in this church. No one else even alive on this planet.

We turn to the priest and that jittery feeling inside me subsides. Like all the things that control fear and nervousness decide once and for all that none of that matters anymore.

My love has been found. My heart is whole. My life is complete.

"Dearly beloved," the priest begins. "We are gathered here today for the shotgun wedding of Emma Dumas and Jesse Boston."

Wait.

What?

"Is everybody ready?"

I put up a hand. "Hold on." I look over my shoulder and see my father holding a gun, pointing it directly at Jesse's back.

He winks at me. "Don't worry, princess. He'll make good."

"What? Dad? What are you doing?"

"Emma?"

I look at Jesse. "What's going on? I'm not pregnant! This isn't a shotgun wedding! It's the dream wedding, remember?"

"Emma?"

"No." I stomp my foot. And when I look down at it, it's not my pretty silver heels encrusted with rhinestones, but the freaking white leather pirate boots. "Where did these come from?"

"Emma?"

I whirl around, stare at my family, gaze homing in on *Karen*. Kraken fuckin' Karen. Why is she here? "You did this, didn't you? Why are you here? Why are you trying to ruin my life?"

"Emma?"

"What?"

"Wake up, babe. Someone's here to talk to us."

I roll over and groan. "No… I'm in the middle of the best dream."

"Emma. Babe. One of the Thumbs is here to talk to us."

My eyes fly open and I sit up.

Well, that's not quite accurate. One eye seems to be stuck together. I reach up to rub it and realize it's being held shut by a sticky fake eyelash. But out of the good, all-the-way-open eye, I see a man. "Oh, no." I flop back down and cover my face with a pillow. "Go away."

"Emma," Jesse says, sitting down on the mattress next to me. "Vinnie says we can have a bonus wedding to make up for the ones that went wrong."

"Nope. Nope. I'm not doing it. The pirate people stole our stuff. We have no clothes, no wallet, no purse, no phones—"

"I'm positive all those things were put away for safekeeping, Miss Dumas," this Vinnie guy says. "We will make sure your clothes and items are all returned."

But I'm not done complaining yet. "My feet hurt, this make-up feels like it's going to take a year to wash off, I don't have a dress, and… yeah. No. I'm over it."

"He promises that this one will be perfect, Ems."

I peek out from under the pillow and see Jesse's handsome, hopeful face. This makes me weak and I relent. A little.

I throw the pillow off me and sit back up. I look at the man standing in the doorway of the jet bedroom. He's a tall, slim man with broad shoulders. Youngish. Maybe late thirties. Handsome in a I-work-for-a-guy-called-Fingers kind of way. And wearing a very expensive and tailored—but a little too shiny—gray Italian suit.

I point my finger at him. "They were all supposed to be perfect. At least… they were not all supposed to be complete disasters! What's it going to be this time? Drive-through wedding chapel? Mmm? And when we get there, they hand us fries and say, 'Sorry. We're all out of weddings?'"

The man folds his hands in front of his waist and smiles at me. Not a toothy grin that personifies the shame he should feel at how badly his boss has ruined our day. But not a placating she's-a-bossy-bridezilla-and-I'm-gonna-placate-her smile, either.

Something in between.

"The Shotgun Wedding, ma'am."

And then my dream comes back to me and I scowl at him. "Shotgun Wedding, huh?"

"It's our biggest, most elaborate fantasy wedding. Picture huge Italian family. Tables and tables of homemade food. A cake seven tiers tall. And the dress.

Oh, the dress..."

"My dress?"

"Uhh..." He pauses. "No. Your dress is... not quite ready."

"Not quite ready? For fuck's sake! The mean little Russian lady said it was gonna take twenty minutes eight hours ago!"

He presses his hands forward in the air in a placating manner. "I understand that. Stasia was a little... let's say, overconfident in her sewing abilities this morning. But we're offering up something better. We've already tailored it to your exact specifications. And no, we hired a special seamstress to handle this one. This is a special *Italian* wedding dress."

I picture every stereotypical Italian wedding I've ever seen in the movies or on TV. "So it's... poofy?"

His mouth falls into a frown. But not a sad frown. Because his head is doing that little bob thing. The this-or-that bob, I like to call it. *Maybe, maybe not,* that bob is saying. Which means yes, it's poofy.

"It's a little bit poofy," he concedes. "But... everything in the Shotgun Wedding package is big. With a capital B. Very over the top. Something you'll remember for the rest of your life, trust me. The chapel is..." He spreads his arms wide. "Gorgeous. Stained-glass windows. Polished-wood pews. Marble floors and painted ceilings. And the people, Miss Dumas. By the time this wedding is over you'll wish these people were *your* people. That's how convincing they are. Fingers will even throw in the extended family for free. You get sisters-in-law, you get brothers-in-law, you get two sets of grandparents, twelve nieces and nephews all dressed for Italian wedding success."

"OK. Hold on." I put up a hand because my brain needs to play catch-up. "So you're saying we get a big, fat, Italian wedding filled with a fake family?"

"Not fake, ma'am. They are a *real* Italian family. Two, in fact. Bride's family and the groom's family. Most of them don't even speak English. Hell, one set of grandparents are straight from Sicily just last summer."

I glance at Jesse. "You really think this is a good idea?"

He shrugs with his shoulders. "We *are* stuck here until Miles and Christopher show back up. We might as well give it another shot."

I peel the fake eyelash off my eyeball, then look down at myself. This stupid pirate dress. The stupid boots. My hair is probably flattened against my head like a helmet from the skull cap and a tangled mess from the skydiving. I sigh. "There's no hope for me today. I'm a complete disaster! Why would I want to get married like this?"

But Vinnie is on it. "We have a spa experience set up at the church, Miss Dumas. You can clean up in a luxurious bubble bath with professional hair and make-up afterward. And your bridesmaids are all color-coordinated. You did choose yellow and peach for your flowers, correct?"

"I did."

"We have that all ready. The whole color scheme is gorgeous. All you have to do is show up, put the dress on, and be the bride you always pictured yourself being."

"Hmm." None of this is what I pictured when I fantasized about my wedding. I don't want a fake family, even if they are real. I want *my* family. "I don't know, Jesse. Maybe this whole thing was a bad idea? Maybe we should just accept the fact that we are wedding failures and go home and let my mother do it her way?"

"Karen Krakken," Jesse says. "Do you really want Karen Krakken as your bridesmaid?"

I sigh.

"We have a photographer, Miss Dumas." Vinnie dangles this in front of me like it's a dog treat.

I narrow my eyes at him. "That's what the pirate wedding guy said. And he was lying about everything."

Vinnie does the head-bob thing again. "The Pick Three is… more of a budget package. A buffet. I believe that word was mentioned when it was explained to you?"

"It was," Jesse admits.

"The Shotgun Wedding is the real deal. We don't do these on the spur of the moment. They take months to plan."

"So let me guess," I say, the cynic inside me still not convinced. "We're going to take someone's place? We're going to be Jack and Elaine for this one? Not Jesse and Emma?"

"No," Vinnie says, again pressing his hands forward in the air. Like he wants to ward off all my well-founded suspicions. "I promise. This one is just for you. Fingers has really gone above and beyond to make sure this one goes off without a hitch."

I look at Jesse. "We're stuck here, babe. We might as well let Fingers make it up to us."

I sigh. "Fine. But this one had better go as planned or I'm… I'm going to… well, I don't really know what I'll do." I point my finger at Vinnie. "But I will do *something*, mister. You can bet on that."

"You have my word, Miss Dumas. This one will go *exactly* as planned."

Vinnie insists that I do not have to clean up before we leave, but I stop at the restroom in the jet lounge anyway and am horrified when I look in the mirror.

Not only do I look like a clown who just went skydiving and then slept on said makeup, my hair is a catastrophe. No wonder that jet lounge lady didn't want to tell me where my jet was! I'm a freak! At this point I don't even care about the wedding. The bath and professional make-up and hair seems like a fair deal for ruining three marriage ceremonies.

But I start to get hopeful that the fourth time might be the charm when, after cleaning up a little in the jet lounge, Vinnie leads us over to a proper limo and not a sparkly purple Fingermobile.

"This is more like it," Jesse says, opening the back door and waiting for me to get in.

"Much better," I agree, sliding in across the soft leather seat. "I might still look like a ragged pirate wench, but the princess package is coming. I can feel it."

He chuckles, sliding in next to me. Then the driver closes the door.

"Wait," I say, putting up a hand. "Where did

216

Vinnie disappear to?"

Jesse turns and looks around through the windows. But nope. No Vinnie. Then he shrugs and settles back into the seat, putting his arm around me. "He's just the coordinator. We don't want him to ride with us anyway."

"Yeah, but every single wedding coordinator so far has also pulled this little disappearing act."

Jesse squeezes my shoulder. "This one will be different. I'm pretty sure Fingers is thinking about all the bad publicity coming his way if Emma Dumas starts telling the world how he cheated us out of our wedding day."

I tsk my tongue. "I'm not gonna badmouth him in public. But I will tell my brothers."

"That would be enough to make me set things right."

My brothers take their sibling responsibilities seriously. Of course, they are much calmer now that we're all grown up, but back when I was a teenager? Yeah, buddy. Anyone who messed with me learned to never do it again. Except Karen Krakken. Because that bitch had a hold of Lonz back then. Normally though, they do swoop in to rescue me any time I need it. They are very suspicious of Jesse and I never even told them about how he broke my heart all those years ago.

So yeah. Fingers should be trying his best to make this right. You do not mess with the Dumas family.

Even though I'm hopeful, I'm super skeptical as the car takes us further and further from the Strip until we're outside the city limits completely and pull into a Santa Fe-style resort with dozens of well-dressed people milling about in front.

"That's them, huh?" I ask, leaning into Jesse to try to get a better look at everything.

"I guess so," he replies.

But there's no time to say anything else because the moment the car stops there's a valet opening his door. Jesse gets out, adjusting his puffy pirate shirt uncomfortably, and then extends his hand to me, and helps me exit with grace. Even though there is absolutely nothing graceful about me in this moment. I'm a hot pirate-wench mess.

Immediately a horde of women attaches themselves to me and *all of them* are speaking Italian. So I have no idea what they are talking about.

I look back at Jesse, and he's being equally monopolized by a group of men. Old, young, even a few teenagers. They have him by the arms and are dragging him off.

"I'll see you at the altar," he yells, smiling big.

I don't know what to say. The women are all

pushing and tugging me off in the complete opposite direction. And then he disappears around the corner of the building and I'm being ushered through a wooden gate and into a small courtyard paved with cobblestones.

The women are all speaking to me. From their tone I can tell they are excited and happy. So I relax and think about the upcoming bubble bath, then hair and makeup. Finally, for the first time today, I will feel special.

Yeah. OK. I'm in. I can do this. Fingers will come through for us and this wedding… it's gonna be the dream wedding. So what if they're not my family? Maybe Vinnie was right? The Shotgun Wedding just might be the golden ticket as far as Vegas elopements go.

Besides, eventually—probably next spring as planned—I'm sure Jesse and I will have the 'real' wedding. And my mother can boss her way through that one all she wants. Who cares? Jesse and I get this one crazy day all to ourselves.

They lead me into a spa. I'm talking there's half a dozen mani-pedi chairs, all of them filled with my new female family members, and a massage table—empty at the moment. But boy, what I wouldn't give for a thirty-minute massage right now. Four ladies doing hair, and yes! A room with a huge circular bathtub filled with bubbles and steam flowing up into the overly-cold air-conditioned room.

I am peeling my clothes off as I walk, that's how good that bath looks. And by the time I get to the other side of the room, I'm naked. In front of strangers. And I don't even care.

One of them—a woman about my age—says something cheerful in Italian and then ushers everyone out and closes the huge double doors behind her.

I dip one foot in the water and groan with happiness. Then climb all the way in and sink down into the hot water with a sigh.

I might never get up.

Everything is wonderful. This whole mess of a day just fades away as I duck my head under and get my hair wet, then reach for the bottles of shampoo off to the side. There are several to consider in pretty, unmarked bottles. I sniff them all and choose one with a faint scent of cherries. It's not overpowering and when I lather it up on my head, the bubbles feel luxurious and thick.

The tub has a handheld sprayer so I rinse and then use a conditioner in a matching bottle. Once that's done, I spend several minutes scrubbing the theatre make-up off my face. And that's when I feel like myself again.

There's a knock at the door almost in that same moment. The same young, pretty woman who ushered everyone out earlier pokes her head in and says something quick and cheerful in Italian.

I have no clue what she's talking about, but this is a wedding and I'm the star attraction. So I assume she's telling me to hurry. She points to a thick, white robe hanging on a peg near the tub and yup. It's time to get out.

As great as the bath felt, I'm ready to get this show on the road. I really think Fingers will come through for us and even though I have a feeling the dress will be a little more… *full* than I imagined in my dream wedding, I'm also confident it will be gorgeous.

This whole place is pretty. And I caught a glimpse of some of the bridesmaids as I was ushered into the bathroom. The dresses were a pale yellow. Very tasteful. Very sophisticated.

Who knows? Maybe I'll love the dress?

I get out, wrap the robe around me, and then step out of the bathroom. The cheerful woman points me over to a chair for hair and four mani-pedi women appear in a swarm and get started on my hands and toes.

I sigh as I look in the mirror, listening intently to

221

the hairdresser as she explains what she's going to do in Italian. Luckily, she uses a lot of hand gestures and I get the gist.

Updo. Nice.

A hair dryer whirls into action as I smile down at my hands and toes, and then close my eyes and enjoy it, thinking, *If Fingers keeps this up, I might have to tip the man.*

I doze a little, still pretty worn out from our crazy adventure. This time yesterday we were just getting ready for the street party.

Shit. I wonder where my family thinks we are? We've definitely been missed at this point. It's nearly four in the afternoon. Note to self: Once the wedding is over, I will call home and explain everything.

My mother will be livid. But she'll get over it. And besides, we'll be home by tomorrow for sure. We have to be home by tomorrow because I have to give Jesse his Christmas present.

Let me tell you, buying presents for a man who has everything? Not easy. I could get him anything he wants. But he could get himself anything he wants too.

So the trick is to get him something he *wants*, but

won't get himself.

I figured out exactly what that was months ago and tomorrow, on Christmas Day, he will be surprised.

I wonder what he'll get me? I'm the same as Jesse. I can afford to buy myself any present I want. But is Jesse clever enough to come up with something I want, but can't buy with money?

We'll see, I guess.

But even if he does get me something material, like a piece of jewelry or a car, or a trip—I don't care. This day, even with all its faults and disappointments, it's one in a million. There's no way we could've planned this crazy adventure.

So I don't care what he gets me for Christmas. As far as I'm concerned, this is my present and I love it.

Yup. This wedding is the one. I'm sure of it.

I really do doze off after that, because the next thing I know I'm being shaken awake. I open my eyes and the woman staring back at me in the mirror is… "Wow!" I smile up at all the ladies. "Wow, you guys! I look amazing!"

And I do. My dark hair is up in a pretty updo with just enough tendrils falling down the side of my face to be artistic, but not messy. And I have a little tiara on my head with a short veil that covers just my eyes.

And my eyes. Wow! They are smoky gray with a little shimmer of bronze and gold, but not depths-of-hell dark like the pirate wedding makeup. My cheeks are the perfect shade of rosy, and my lips are the perfect glistening pink.

I nod in approval and clap my hands. "I love it!" I beam at them and they beam back. "So great, you guys!"

Then they're urging me up and leading me over to… "Holy shit!" That dress is spectacular. No, I wasn't imagining a poofy Cinderella dress with layers and layers of tulle and off-the-shoulder-satin for sleeves when I pictured my fantasy wedding, but… I'm not complaining about *this*. It's a million times better than anything the mean Russian Stasia could come up with, that's for sure!

A whole crew bustles around me, helping me put on the corset lingerie, tying me up tight, but not too tight. These girls really know what they're doing.

But what do I expect? They are professional bridesmaids, I guess.

I put the garters and stocking on, thinking that Mr. Boston is really gonna get a neat little treat when he finally gets to lift my dress up afterward. Then they help me step into the gown.

Because that's what this is. Not a dress, a gown. With more underskirts than I'd prefer, but when they spin me around after hooking up all the buttons in the back, and I see myself in the mirror—holy shit, yes. Yes! This is what Emma Dumas, the Bossy Bride, should look like!

But I only have a few moments to appreciate myself in the mirror before the music starts playing somewhere outside and everyone starts chattering away in Italian.

I figure this is my cue.

It's time to get married.

I let them bustle me outside and back into the courtyard. Then they grab my hands and we move forward as a team towards the chapel.

And Vinnie was right. The chapel is gorgeous. And that's just the outside of it. Its white walls with artfully placed patches of crumbling plaster make it look like something built hundreds of years ago. It has quaint wooden shutters painted a pale blue that matches the sky above us. The steps are a wide, gently sloping half circle leading up to the double front doors.

The sweet scent of peonies and roses—in yellow and peach—fills the air as I follow them up the steps and stand in the doorway.

The music changes and the Bride's March begins. And I am desperate—simply *desperate*—to see past all of my bridesmaids and get a peek at my handsome, charming, perfect groom.

The ladies shuffle around and pair off, then they start their walk. The little flower girl hops in front of me like this is her big moment, not mine.

An older man appears on my right. He's dressed in a very nice black tux. He says something in Italian to me and offers me his arm.

Damn. Fingers went all out. He got me a stand-in father.

But… I have to admit, I really do wish it was my real father escorting me down the aisle.

He says a few words that I interpret as, *Are you ready?*

I nod. And then we begin to walk.

That's when I look up at the altar and see Jesse Boston in a fancy black and gray tux in contrasting colors—wearing a top hat!—hands folded in front of him, and grinning at me like… *Yup, babe. Fourth time really is the charm.*

He looks like a billion Boston bucks.

CHAPTER FIFTEEN

When the wedding music starts and the fake bridesmaids start lining up at the chapel door, it all becomes real. And even though this is the fourth time today Emma and I have been through the start of a wedding, this is the first time that I get proper butterflies.

The rollercoaster wedding wasn't even ours. It was fun to be on the ride and I guess if we'd been the real bride and groom, that sick nervous feeling I had at the top of the first hill would've counted as butterflies. But it wasn't our wedding and so that feeling was just the anticipation of the wild ride to come.

Which, now that I think back on it, could be interpreted literally.

The pirate wedding wasn't a wedding but a show and if I had known it was a show, I'd have been properly nervous about it. But we had no clue what was happening. It kinda pissed me off when I realized it was a scam and we were not even going to get married at the end, but looking back on it now—hell, I was kind of badass swinging on those ropes trying to save Emma from all those hot, shirtless pirate dudes.

The skydiving wedding did give me butterflies, but not in a I'm-about-to-marry-the-love-of-my-life way. More of a I'm-gonna-die-in-the-next-thirty-seconds way.

This wedding though? This is how it's done. As soon as we arrived and she was whisked off one way, and I was dragged off another, it was different. These fake Italian family members are really invested in this wedding. I have six groomsmen. All my age, all pretty good-looking dudes. And now that I see the bridesmaids coming down the aisle, I'm confident our wedding pictures will be amazing. I'm talking wedding planner brochure kind of amazing. I would not be surprised if Fingers uses our ceremony photographs to sell this Shotgun Wedding package in the future.

I spent most of the day second-guessing our spur-of-the-moment decision to elope in Vegas, but I'm pretty satisfied now.

Of course, that has a lot to do with the groom treatment I got while Emma was off getting ready. All of my groomsmen were very determined that I enjoy all the things waiting for me in the little groom cottage.

It was set up like a gentleman's study. Think dark paneled walls, leather chairs and couches, a polished bar with every kind of top-shelf alcohol you can think of. They even had cigars.

I did puff a cigar for a little bit, just trying to relax after our crazy day. Of course, I didn't drink, but that's OK. They did enough of that for me.

They laughed and talked to me in Italian like I could understand them. And I nodded and smiled and just generally kicked back in a huge leather chair.

Then we all went into the steam room. I've never been a guy who likes a steam, but I have to admit it was a very nice touch. My sore muscles certainly thanked me afterward. We just sat in there for a good twenty minutes and I listened to them all talk. They're very animated, these Italian dudes. And they all kinda look alike, so I think they're really family.

The first three weddings were pretty cheesy, but this one... *An A-plus effort, Fingers, my man. A-fucking-plus.*

After the steam I took a long, cool shower and when I got out, there was a barber there to give me a proper shave. I'm talking this dude oiled me up, wrapped a lemon-scented hot towel all the way round my head to relax me, and then worked that shaving cream into my jaw until I had a fluffy cloud on my face. He skimmed that straight-cut razor down my jaw like an expert, gave me a face-wash mask, hot-toweled me again, cleaned off the mask, and then massaged some post-shave balm and moisturizer into my baby's-butt-smooth skin so thoroughly, I felt like a new man.

He even trimmed and styled my hair.

Then they showed me the tux.

I have to admit, I was a little worried it was going to be shiny and cheap, but Fingers pulled through for me with a charcoal-gray jacket with tails and matching slacks, light gray waistcoat, white shirt with light gray pinstripes, and a yellow tie. Not what I would've chosen for my wedding day. It's a little bit contrast-y for my tastes and it came with a top hat. But that's kind of the cool thing about letting other people make choices for you. You get what you get and even if it's not really 'you', you can embrace it because it wasn't your choice.

I decide I love the suit and when I see all my groomsmen lined up before we walk, I think we look damn good.

None of them speak English. Or so they say. But they come with names like Marco, and Giovanni, and Leonardo, and I actually start picturing myself with these dudes as my buddies. I could use a few buddies. I wonder if the Shotgun Wedding is their day job or if they have other careers? I start picturing Marco as a finance guy in the city. He's a fast talker with a loud voice and lots of hand gestures. Leonardo is slim and blond and comes off as an artist, moody and quiet. I picture him agonizing over color choice in his paintings. And in my head, Giovanni is some kind of professor. Probably history. Probably weird history. Like… gladiators. Or Vikings. Or the Persian Wars.

Yeah. I like my new friends. I could see myself hanging out with these guys.

There's even a little dude called Edwardo who is gonna carry our rings.

Haven't seen the rings yet, but from the looks of this wedding so far, I'm fairly confident that they'll be expensive and maybe even tasteful. Hell, we might even keep them. I'm sure Fingers will mark them up two hundred percent, but you can't put a price on memories, right?

Well, you can. I know this because Joey, Huck, Wald, and Brooke bought a whole lifetime of memories when they were trying to get custody of Maisy. But that's not the point. I think we'll probably keep the rings. I think this wedding is gonna be something we'll want to remember for the rest of our lives.

There's some fussing at the chapel entrance as the bridesmaids begin their walk and then... there. There she is. My bride.

I start grinning like a madman. I can't help it. I'm bobbing my head from side to side, trying to see past all the bridesmaids—and then... well, shit. Then I actually catch myself looking for Jack. Because he should be the one walking her down the aisle.

Now... *now* I feel bad about this wedding.

Jack should be here. Silvia should be sitting right up front where that middle-aged Italian mother-in-law stand-in is. And even though I kinda dig Marco, Giovanni, Leonardo, and Edwardo—it should be Joey and Johnny standing up here with me. Huck and Wald too. And fuckin' Lonz. And Tony and Luke and...

Fuck. Fuck! My best man should be Zach!

But just as that regret begins to simmer in my head, the bridesmaids all make it to the altar and the wedding march begins. A little flower girl appears, tossing peach and yellow flower petals—and dammit, that flower girl should be Maisy.

But then...

"Holy shit," I mutter. Because I see Emma. Emma. My bride. Not dressed up in jeans and t-shirt like she was for the rollercoaster wedding, not dressed up like a pirate princess like she was at Treasure Island, not dressed up in a jumpsuit at the skydiving wedding—but dressed up like a proper I'm-gonna-lose-my-shit she's-the-most-beautiful-bride-ever kind of bride.

Her dress is… a little Cinderella. And I know she probably wouldn't have chosen that style if we were in charge of this day, but it's beautiful. And she looks gorgeous. All of the day's catastrophes have been washed off and her face is bright with happiness.

Marco elbows me, muttering something in Italian I can only assume is probably along the lines of, *Your woman is sexy hot and I bet the lingerie she's wearing underneath is gonna blow your mind* , but I can't even shoot him a disapproving glare, because he's right.

My bride is sexy hot.

And no, the man whose arm she's holding onto as she walks isn't her father. And none of these people here are our people—but in this moment I do not care.

Emma.

Emma is the only thing on my mind.

I want this woman by my side *right now*. I want her next to me for the rest of my life. I want her in sickness and in health. I'll take all the bad with the good. I want to love and cherish her so hard, she will forget the thirteen years we spent apart and only think of the ones we spent together.

Her veil only covers her eyes. It's a very tasteful, very understated veil. But the best thing about that veil is that as I watch her walk towards me—as I see her suddenly realize that this is it, we really are gonna make it all the way through this ceremony—I catch her checking me out. I catch her eyes wandering down my body, then back up to meet my gaze again.

She smiles and bites her lip.

And man, that little lip-biting thing? Yeah. I'm gonna picture that every time I make love to her for the rest of my life.

My stomach flips with excitement once they reach the steps and all I want to do is rush down those steps and pull her into my arms.

But I wait.

I force myself to stand still and wait as her fake father pauses to look lovingly at her—nice touch, fake father-in-law—and then she ascends towards me.

Emma's eyes find mine as she slowly approaches the altar. And then she shrugs up her shoulders as if a tingle went up her body.

God, I love her. I love her so much. And even though I still have regrets about missing out on all those years when we were apart, I know—I just feel it in my heart—that this is just the beginning for us. We have so much to look forward to. And pretty soon none of those missing years will matter anymore. We'll be too busy making new memories to even think about the ones we never had.

When they reach the top her fake father stops just a step away from me, turns to Emma, and lifts her small veil up and says something low and soft in Italian.

Emma nods her head at him and murmurs, "Thank you."

Then she turns to me. I reach for her and she takes my hand, stepping forward to stand next to me as we both face each other in front of this chapel filled with people.

It's only then that we realize… the priest is speaking in Italian.

Both of us giggle. Fuck it, right?

What did we really expect? And surely, this day could not get any weirder.

We hold hands as he speaks, probably saying all the usual things. Marriage is serious. Marriage is a lifelong commitment. Marriage is sacred.

Yes. I agree to all those things.

I hold Emma's hands in mine as the ceremony proceeds. And I even hear a sniffle or two from our audience. *Nice touch, Fingers. Nice touch.*

And even though everything here started out fake, suddenly everything feels very, *very* real.

I am marrying this woman.

The priest pauses, and when we look at him we realize we're up.

We didn't discuss this. We have no vows! And even though everyone else is working off a script, we're just winging it.

Emma looks a little frightened. Her eyes are wide and her pouty lips are making a perfect, round, o shape.

I squeeze her hand. "I got you, babe." Then I clear my throat and begin.

"Emma Dumas. I first met you thirteen years ago. We were young, and one of us was very stupid." She smiles wide and sucks in a breath of air. "Me," I say, looking out at the crowd. And hey, they get it. Because they chuckle a little at my joke. "But I don't think I ever told you how you grabbed my attention that day. I saw you from across Mallory Square. You were wearing little Daisy Duke cut-offs and a white tank top. And, of course, those now infamous pigtails."

She squeezes my hands as she shakes her head and looks down for a moment. But she quickly raises her eyes back up to meet mine. Like she refuses to miss a single moment of our big minute.

"And Emma, I thought to myself... 'Jesse Boston—'" A slight murmur from the crowd makes me pause for a moment. I guess they didn't know who

I was and now they do. Jesse Boston is the same no matter what language you say it in. "I said, 'Jesse Boston, how in the heck have you been on this island for a week and are just now seeing this girl?' You see," I say to the crowd, "I missed her. And I hated that. I really hated that. Because up until that moment when I first saw this vision of a girl, I was doing nothing. I *was* nothing. I was wasting time, and taking up space, and couldn't even begin to imagine what the next thirteen minutes would bring, let alone the next thirteen years. So I took my chance." I turn back to Emma. "I went up to your shaved ice stand and asked you out. It was probably not my best pick-up. But Emma, I just want you to know... it was my most honest one."

She lowers her eyes again. And when they rise up to meet mine just a moment later, I see the shine of a tear in them.

"It was... *honest*. Every moment with you that night was honest. And when we reconnected thirteen years later, every moment that came after was honest too. You not only make me want to be a better man, I am a better man with you by my side." I bring her hand up to my lips and I gently kiss her fingers. "Thank you. Thank you for seeing the better me. Thank you for buying me from a bachelor auction with grand delusions of revenge. Thank you for the one-up dream date. Thank you for sharing your family with me. Thank you for being my knight in shining armor... just..." I shake my head. "Babe? I can't do this without you."

She inhales deeply, lets go of one of my hands to swipe a tear off her cheek, and then says, "Jesse Boston. You were my fantasy man when we first met. You were the man who made all the promises. You were a boy so golden I could barely stand to look at you."

I sigh. Because I didn't feel good enough for her back then. I was so afraid she'd see through me. So afraid she'd realize what a fraud I was. So afraid that she'd figure me out and sneak away, thankful that she dodged a bullet with a boy called Jesse.

"And when you disappeared, I was lost. I was someone else when you left. Some other girl who no longer understood her place in this world. And for the next thirteen years I would think about you at least once a day. I would think... what could we have been? What life would we have lived if we had stayed together from the start? If we had never gone out and did our thing, by ourselves, on our own?" She squeezes my hands. "And you know what?"

"What?" I whisper, dying to know what she thinks

about this.

"We might've been *that* couple."

I laugh a little. *That* couple.

"We might have been that couple you described on our second-chance first date last summer. The one who fights hard, and lives fast, and loves each other ferociously."

"Love is a battlefield, babe. And we're both just generals."

She giggles. "That's right. It's a pretty romantic idea. But you know what's even more romantic?"

"I think you're about to tell me."

"Us. The real us. That's even more romantic than the fantasy us. Because the real us, Jesse Boston—the real us is strong. The real us is smart. The real us is resilient. The real us is… well…" She shrugs with her shoulders. "We're real, Jesse. And I know all this is fake. This whole day was set up to be something fake. Every bit of this day was a crazy fantasy. But I just want you to know that this moment? This one right now? This is all us, Baby Boston. I don't care who's sitting in this chapel with us. I don't care that we don't know them, and they don't know us, and this isn't my dress, and that isn't your tux. It's real. Because this moment is about my love for you and that's the only thing that counts."

She and I both suck in a deep breath of air and suddenly the world is… different. Better. Brighter. Realer than real.

Because she's right. This moment, and the ones that come next, those are the only ones that count. "I love you, Emma Dumas."

"I love you back, Jesse Boston."

I turn to the priest and nod. "And that's all there is."

He smiles at us. Maybe he understands the actual words of our impromptu vows or maybe he's done this enough to just feel the meaning of our moment. But his smile is big. His arms go up and he spreads them wide, opens his mouth and tells me to kiss my bride in a language I don't understand, and then the chapel doors swing open with a bang.

Everyone gasps and turns around to see who dares interrupt our moment of bliss.

I squint my eyes at the man standing in the doorway, unable to figure out who it is or why he's there.

And then there is chaos.

CHAPTER SIXTEEN

Chaos.

Total and utter chaos.

Everyone stands up. People are shouting. The groomsmen all pull out guns from their suit coats. My bridesmaids are running to the back of the altar, trying to hide.

My fake mother is screaming. I'm talking this little round lady is yelling at the top of her Italian lungs. My fake father suddenly has like... a machine gun or whatever you call them, and then, from behind the guy who just stopped the wedding, there's a whole other group of men silhouetted in the doorway. All are dressed up in black suits. All have guns out.

I roll my eyes and look at Jesse.

"For fuck's sake," he says, running his fingers through his hair. "Are you kidding me right now? I mean, Fingers! Dude!" He yells it to the ceiling like maybe, hopefully, there's some hidden cameras up there and Fingers will magically hear his plea and stop this mess before it gets out of hand. Like maybe there's a way to just kiss, get back to the whole 'I now pronounce you husband and wife. You may kiss the bride' moment and pretend this surprise twist didn't happen. "We were so close, man! This isn't necessary!"

But then the shooting starts. The mobster guy in the doorway is screaming. And blazing guns aside, there's no possible way to miss that these are threats.

At first, I figure it's all part of the show, right? This is Treasure Island all over again, but with mobsters. I mean, the name of the package *is* Shotgun Wedding.

But Jesse's right. We do not need the theatrics. We've had enough. So we just stand there for a moment, totally convinced this is fake.

Until my fake father-in-law takes a bullet to the chest, twists in the air, and falls flat on his face.

I just kinda stare at him for a moment, still thinking this is fake. It's a good fake. I'll give them that. It's pretty authentic. But it's not real.

It cannot be real.

But then I see the exit wound in his back, and the blood pooling on the floor around his upper body, and then two things happen simultaneously.

I scream. I don't even know where that scream comes from, it's like instinct.

And then someone from the Mob family yells, "Jesse motherfucking Boston!"

And then another thing happens.

Jesse and I look at the man screaming his name, then at each other, and then he's running. He's got my hand, and we're running. Past the now shooting back groomsmen, past the podium thingy in the center of the altar, and through a gold curtain that leads to some chapel back room.

"What the fuck was that?" I yell. Maybe this isn't Fingers? Maybe this is about the Boston brothers?

But Jesse is still running, still tugging me along behind him. He finds a door, slams into the silver crossbar to open it, and it goes swinging out so fast it bangs into the side of the building. Then we're running along the side of the chapel to the back as a full-on shootout happens inside.

"Jesus fucking Christ!" Jesse yells. "I'm gonna kill Miles, and Fingers, and Clarence, and Steve, and Jessica, and Sven, and Vinnie, and—"

But he stops short. Because we've reached the rear parking lot and there's a whole other gang of men back here. They see us and yell, "There he is!" In English, too. So that's our second clue that these guys might not be Fingers' guys. They might, in fact, be real guys after Jesse Boston. Because while I was making fun of his so-called mobster connections this morning, the truth is, Jesse *is* part of some kind of Mob. It might not be the fake family inside the chapel kind of Mob, but it's still a secret criminal organization. And yeah, there might actually be people upset with the Boston brothers right now. We never did get the whole story out of Johnny when he came back from the Caribbean with a weird science girl called Megan and no Charlotte Kane.

"This way!" Jesse yells, already running back to the front of the church. I'm definitely out of my element here, so I'm really thankful that he's got a hold of my hand and is still dragging me behind him, because without that direction I would probably still be standing in that rear parking lot with a sick, confused look on my face.

Instead, I'm now running past the front of the church where there are lots of haphazardly parked black SUVs with blackout windows. And there might even be a whole other army of mobsters inside them, but we don't stop. We head to the one car we know is empty.

The 'Just Married' car, complete with tin cans painted peach and yellow and a giant peach satin bow affixed to each door handle.

It's a sporty little Mercedes convertible in pale yellow. A classic, actually. Something very vintage Grace Kelly. Something I'd drive if I were living like a princess in Monaco and not the CFO of Bright Berry Beach Cosmetics.

But then Jesse is shoving me into the car, my dress flying up over my head as I crash into the seat. And he's climbing over me, turning the key in the ignition as I upright myself and paw layers and layers of tulle out of my face.

Fucking Cinderella dress!

But then again… my mind is suddenly trying to picture all this going down in a mermaid dress and I think the Cinderella dress actually works better in this particular situation. I don't think I could've uprighted myself in a mermaid dress and right now Jesse Boston would be driving out of this rural resort with my ass in the air.

Which makes me chuckle. Because my rambling train of thought is insane. Hell, the whole fucking thing is insane!

The tin cans are making a huge ruckus behind us and I take a moment to plot a scheme in which I climb over the back and somehow unhook the cans, but then I realize that's a level of insane I'm not willing to descend to and look forward again.

I yell, "Stop!"

Because Jesse is looking back at the cans too, and right in the middle of the fucking exit of the resort is a woman blocking the road.

Jesse slams on the brake and we both jerk forward. The car stops within inches of the woman, who I now realize is Karen fucking Krakken.

I say, "Karen?" Because… how the fuck? What the fuck? Who the fuck? All the fucks! None of this makes any sense at all and for a moment I wonder if I'm asleep back in the bridal dressing room. Like… that tub of hot bubbles felt so good I just passed out and all of this is just some Fingers' Fantasy Wedding Pick Three Buffet-induced dream.

But no. She's real.

Kraken Karen runs towards our car and yells, "Quick! Get out and come with me!"

I say nothing. I'm too stunned. I'm still trying to make all these square pegs fit into round holes.

But Jesse is on it. He says, "Fuck you, bitch!" and backs up. Then he shifts the car back into first and we peel out, sliding right around Kraken Karen, and then ten seconds later we're going eighty down the totally empty, abandoned desert road towards the sunset.

I yell, "Oh, my fucking God!" and then, "Where

are we going?"

And Jesse yells back—because the wind is pretty loud in a convertible—"We're going home! Right the fuck now. I don't care if we have to drive this car all the way to Florida, we're outta here!"

He speeds off down the road, but there are a few switchbacks and that slows us down. The cherry on top of this day will not be the both of us going over the side of a dusty desert mountain Grace Kelly-style.

"Is anyone following us?"

I turn to look around, but we're on a curve and the mountain is in the way. But then... I see them. Headlights across the canyon on another switchback. The black SUVs. "Yes! Holy shit! They are!"

"How far back?"

"Maybe half a mile!"

He goes a little faster and I can see this ending coming. I swear to God. We're going over the side of the cliff.

But what I don't see until it's almost too late is the big black van coming towards us from the other direction.

"Shit!" Jesse yells, turning the wheel to the left. The car slides to the right and almost turns completely around.

And that's when the train of black SUVs comes

around the last switchback.

"What do we do?" I ask. My heart is pounding inside my chest, adrenaline coursing through my body. Is this part of the wedding? Is this real? Will these people hurt us—or, even worse, will they hurt Jesse and leave me alone?

The thought of something happening to him, or me, or us—that's bad. But the idea that I might have to go on without him? That's so much worse. I can't do it. I won't do it.

The SUVs come to a stop about fifty yards away and when I check behind us, the black van is only about ten.

We're trapped between them and the only way out that doesn't involve being shoved in the back of a black van is to go over the side of the road and run.

"Let's run," I say, nearly breathless from the panic building inside me.

"Run where?" Jesse asks. "This has to be a joke, right? This has Fingers written all over it, don't you think? Shotgun Wedding?"

"Maybe. But"—I caution him—"this could be about you. Or Joey. Johnny. Or hell, Brooke and Megan are caught up in all this crap too. It could be about *us*, Jesse."

"Mr. Boston," a singsong voice calls from one of

the stopped SUVs.

And yup. That pretty much solves that mystery. It is about us. This isn't some crackpot fantasy wedding. I mean, who the hell would pay good money for that beautiful wedding only to have mobsters come in and shoot it all up before you even say 'I do'?

"You found me," Jesse yells back. He's calm and cool. Like this is just another chance meeting with some old friends.

The passenger side door of the closest SUV opens and a tall man in a black suit and dark sunglasses slides out while buttoning his jacket. Other men get out after him, all of them pointing guns at us.

Do these men want to hurt us?

Why the hell was Kraken Karen at the resort?

Did I imagine her? Am I just making shit up after a day filled with more make-believe than I can handle? Or was that really her?

Is she being used by the Way? Did someone from the Boston brothers' secret Mob organization find her and think, *Hey, let's use Kraken Karen to get to Emma and Jesse?* Or is she in on this? Is Karen Krakken Channing part of the Way?

Off in the distance I hear the thumping sound of a helicopter. We all hear it at the same time and everyone glances up at the sky for a moment.

Is that the cops? More mobsters? Some secret Fingers Thumb team ready to swoop in like the cavalry? Will we get pulled to safety at the last second and then have a good laugh?

You got us again! Joke's on us! Haha. Fuckin' Fingers! He sure knows how to throw a fantasy Shotgun Wedding!

But no. The helicopter never materializes and a few seconds later even the thumping of the rotors disappears.

"Well?" Jesse yells. "What do you want?"

The man is silent for a minute. "Here's what I want, Mr. Boston. You see that van behind you?"

We know the van is behind us, but we both look over our shoulders instinctively.

"I want you two to walk towards that van with your hands in the air. And once you reach those men, they are going to tie you up and you're going to be very good and cooperate."

"Look." Jesse sighs like he's tired. "We know this is all part of the wedding—"

"What wedding?" the man in black asks.

Jesse lets out an incredulous huff. "What wedding? Uh, the one we just *escaped* from?" He does air quotes for the word 'escaped.'

The man in black just stares at Jesse impassively.

"Hello?" Jesse calls. "My bride?" He points to me.

"She's wearing a big, poofy wedding dress. I'm in coattails? Any of this sounding familiar to you?"

"Sir," the man says, and he sounds tired too. "Where you were and what you were doing before we stopped you here is none of my concern."

Jesse looks at me. We make confused faces at each other. Then he looks back at the man in black. "Then… what is your concern?"

"Some people would like to talk to you. I was sent to pick you up."

"What people?" Jesse asks.

"I'm afraid that's above my pay grade. Now let's get back to the van."

"No," Jesse says. He pushes me behind him and puts his hands out in front of him. "We're not going anywhere until you tell us who sent you."

But then one of the SUV thugs points a gun in the air and shoots it. I jump and maybe even squeal a little, because it was loud and I was not expecting that.

"What the fuck!" Jesse yells. "What the fuck is going on?"

The shooter pops off another warning shot.

The man in black lowers his sunglasses down the bridge of his nose, and glares at Jesse. "Get in the fucking van, Jesse Boston. You're the last one on our list today. We've already got your brothers in custody and if you ever want to see them or their loved ones alive again, you'd better start cooperating."

And I swear to God the entire desert goes silent in the aftermath of that revelation.

CHAPTER SEVENTEEN

JESSE

Emma just stares at me.

And I get it. This is stupid. This can't be real. There's a major part of my brain still insisting that this is all fake.

But there's plenty of reasons why this *could* be real. We are the fuckin' Boston brothers. We have more money than God. We're part of some super-secret organization that does who knows what, all over the globe. And people kinda love to hate me.

But some of this makes no sense.

I could actually see Joey getting himself caught by some thugs if he was alone and not with his partners. But Johnny? There is no way that Johnny Boston would allow himself to get caught. He's too smart. Too ruthless. Too suspicious of pretty much everyone.

But... coming home with Megan and moving out

of the Bossy resulted in a major upset in his normally super-tight security protocols. And, though I hate to admit this, if people want to get to Johnny Boston now, all they have to do is grab Megan. Especially since she's pregnant.

He would flip out if someone got a hold of Megan. Or hell, they could just grab his new puppy. He loves that crazy puppy.

Megan and Jasper are Johnny's weaknesses just like Emma is mine. Just like Wald, and Huck, and Brooke, and Maisy are Joey's.

So… this *could* be real. They might actually have Joey and Johnny somewhere. They could have Megan, and Brooke, and Huck, and Wald too.

We could be fucked.

Mr. Boston. That's what they're calling me. And those fake people back in the chapel… they did react when they heard my last name.

Yeah. This is about the Bostons. I can feel it in my bones.

"OK," I finally say.

We get out of the car.

Emma is stunned and just stares at me, unable to move. So I take her hands, raise them up, and then turn her around and point her in the direction of the van. "We're walking."

"This has to be a joke. Right?" she pleads.

I turn my head to look at her, not sure what to say. "I don't know, Emma. But I'm not going to take any chances. Not when it comes to you. I'm sorry."

"For what?"

"For dragging you into my stupid, fucked-up life. If you weren't with me none of this would be happening to you."

She huffs. "Don't be ridiculous. It's got to be fake."

"Well, if it is... then why are those two dudes next to the van holding zip ties and black hoods?"

"Oh, my God," she whispers. "We're gonna die."

"We're not. Well, *you're* not. Whatever they want, I'll give it to them. They want me? Fine. They can have me if they let you go."

"Fine?" she hisses. "No! That's not fine. We were married four times today. What part of that whole 'till death do us part' thing don't you understand?"

"Well... not to be a buzzkill here, but we didn't actually get married at any of those weddings, Emma."

"It doesn't matter! It's the thought that counts! We stood up four times in front of people with the intention of being married! It *counts*!"

We reach the men. They spin us around and zip-tie our hands and then drop the hoods over our heads. We're walked forward and we climb into the back of the van. There are no seats or anything, so we back up against the side and lean into each other.

The doors slam closed and then there's nothing but silence. A few seconds later the van jostles back and forth as the driver gets in. Then we're moving.

There's no way to tell which direction we're headed or where we're going. And for a long while there's no real road noise either. But then eventually it becomes clear that we're back in the city. Whether this is Vegas or not remains to be seen, I guess. But there's stop-and-go traffic, and long waits at stoplights, and lots of turning.

Then we're going downward and Emma has to brace herself against me so she doesn't fall over. The tires squeal with a familiar and distinct echo as we spiral down a ramp.

"A parking garage," Emma whispers. "I think we're in a parking garage."

I think she's right. This can't be good.

The van stops and almost immediately someone is opening the doors and pulling us out. They say nothing. And even though I want to ask all the questions, there's no point. They were probably instructed to be quiet and just bring us in.

All we can do is walk. Someone has a firm grip on my arm, leading me along a long hallway. I can hear people. I feel like we're close to a very crowded place. A casino, probably. But which one? I consider yelling. Calling for help. But the low murmur of people isn't that close. It almost feels like we're in a separate part of a building. If I called out no one would hear me. Well, no one except for the person who has a hold of my arm.

I force myself to be calm. Once they take the hood off and we know where we are, I can try to negotiate.

Maybe they only want money?

God, I hope they only want money.

We enter a new room filled with the sounds of generators. Maybe AC units or something similar. All I know is that the crowd hum is gone and in its place is the white noise of machinery.

We stop.

We wait.

The person who had a hold of my arm lets go and then I can hear the faint sound of footsteps over the noise in the room.

"Hey!" I call.

"Oh, my God," Emma says. "What's happening? Did they just leave us here?"

But then someone is behind me. I try to turn around, but another person grabs my shoulder.

Strong hands grab my shoulders, holding me still,

and I think to myself... *This is it. It all ends here. In Vegas, after a crazy day of weddings where we never actually managed to get married. In some dark, kinda stinky room that reminds me of...*

Wait.

"The ocean?" I say.

"Yeah," Emma says. "I smell it too."

Then the zipties around my wrists are cut and the hood is pulled off my head.

It takes me several whole seconds to take in where I am and what I'm looking at.

"An aquarium?"

And that's when I see Cowboy Clarence smiling and rocking back and forth on his heels like he's just pulled off the wedding of the century.

"What the hell?" I say.

"Mr. and Mrs. Boston," Clarence starts.

I'm about to say something about that—including all the ways in which we are so not Mr. and Mrs. Boston right now—but Emma beats me to it.

"Uh. No!" she exclaims. "We are *not* Mr. and Mrs. Boston because you—you slimy, cheating, filthy, lying cowboy!—you ruined every single wedding we tried to have today!"

Clarence presses his hands forward, like he's trying to ward off Emma's upcoming rage.

But I'm with Emma. "What the actual fuck, dude? We were literally two seconds away from saying 'I do' back at the Shotgun Wedding when your... stupid Mob boss barged in and ruined it!"

"Now, listen—" Clarence starts.

"No, you listen!" Emma yells. "We missed Christmas Eve dinner with our family because of you! We are stuck in Las Vegas when we should be in Key West because of you! That rollercoaster wedding wasn't even for us! The pirate wedding was actually not a wedding, but a stupid show. And by the way, my almost-husband could've been killed swinging from those ropes trying to save me." She air-quotes the 'save me' part, which I kinda love. "Then you throw us out of a plane and... and what? Did you fuck up the mics on purpose? I don't get it! You make no sense! Then you send Cousin Vinnie to talk us into the perfect, over-the-top Italian Wedding, which, also by the way, I loved. And then you ruin everything by sending in some Mob boss to kill everyone!"

"They're not dead," Clarence explains. "It was all fake!"

"*I knew it was fake!*" Emma screams. She's pissed. "That's even worse! Because we thought we were running for our lives! I was so... so... kerfluffled, I actually hallucinated my childhood nemesis, Kraken—

"

She stops.

Because—what the fuck?—Kraken Karen walks out from the shadows and smiles at Emma. Actually has the nerve to *smile* at her!

"Not a hallucination," the Kraken quips. "That was all my idea!"

Emma lunges at her, hands out in a choking gesture, like she's about to wrap them around Karen's throat.

I grab her arm just in time and pull her into me. Hug her tight. Because I'm pretty sure Emma is gonna murder that chick.

"Your *idea*!" Emma screams. "I will kill you with my bare hands for ruining my wedding! Are you that small and self-obsessed that you had to ruin our whole day just because we didn't want you to plan our wedding and fuck up my wedding photos with your Kraken face? God, you are such a bitch! You really need to get a life!"

"OK, hold on here."

All of us turn to look at another man standing off to the side. It's the man-in-black dude who ordered us to get in the van back in the desert.

"You," I say. "Who the fuck *are* you?"

"I," the man says, pointing to his chest, "am

Fingers." He takes a little bow and then smiles at me. "At your service."

And now Emma is the one holding me back, because this is the actual asshole responsible for everything today.

This is the asshole who deserves to be choked out and I'm going to be the one to do it.

And that's when a mermaid on a swing begins to descend from the ceiling...

CHAPTER EIGHTEEN

"Mila?" I exclaim. And I have to admit, I'm a little shrieky at the moment. The sound of my voice makes everyone cringe. Even me.

"Oh, my fucking God." Mila laughs. "You two are crazy!"

"What the hell are you doing? And why are you dressed up like a mermaid?"

"Uh…" Mila laughs. "Hello? Earth to Emma? I'm your maid of honor."

"What?" I'm so confused. But then there are two more swings being lowered from the ceiling. And two more mermaids, swinging their tails back and forth like this is all good fun. "Hannah? Natalie! What in God's name is *happening*?"

"Stop hogging the spotlight, Mila!" Natalie says as her swing lowers. "All three of us are your bridesmaids,

Ems."

"I'm so disappointed in you," Hannah says, kicking her tail. "I cannot believe you were actually going to have a wedding without us!"

"What?" I look at Jesse. I'm stunned.

But he just laughs. Then he points to Fingers and says, "Well played, Mr. Fingers. Well played."

Fingers holds up his hands again. "I'm afraid none of this was my idea."

I look at Karen. "You? You really did all this?"

Karen shrugs her shoulders all the way up to her ears. "Well, I would love to take credit for all of it, but I'm afraid it wasn't my original idea."

"It was ours."

I turn to look behind me and see my mother, arm in arm with Miles. "You two?"

Jesse barks out a laugh. "What?"

My mom lets go of Miles and walks towards me. She takes both my hands in hers and gives them a tight squeeze. "Miles told me you were upset that I was bossing you out of your perfect wedding. He called us before you left for Vegas. And then…" She beams a smile at me. "We decided that if you wanted a crazy Vegas wedding, we'd make it happen."

And then my father and all three of my brothers walk out from behind a large air compressor.

"Are you kidding me right now?" I can't help it, I practically cackle.

"Cowboy Clarence?" Tony says. "That was my idea."

"And the rollercoaster?" Luke says. "I came up with that one."

I look at Alonzo. "And you?"

He opens his hands wide and says, "Fuckin' pirates! They're pretty much the answer to everything. And"—he eyeballs Jesse with a big-brother glare—"the skydiving was a given."

"You tried to kill me, didn't you?" Jesse points an accusatory finger at my massive, tatted-up brother.

Alonzo scowls at him. "Hey. You lived, right?"

"I planned the Shotgun Wedding," Karen quips, trying to defuse the brewing almost-brother-in-law rivalry. "Your mom was worried you'd both bail out before we could get all the arrangements for the aquarium ready, so I came up with something more... traditional."

"Traditional?" I blink at her. "There was a shootout at the end!"

"Well, we couldn't let you actually get married before the aquarium was ready," Luke says. "Duh, Emma."

"I tried to stop you two from leaving," Karen says.

"The kidnapping wasn't actually part of the plan. We were just going to tell you after the shootout once we had you in the SUV's, but then you stole the wedding car and we were afraid you'd get away and miss your big moment. So Fingers agreed to get his men in on this and take over."

"We didn't know which crazy wedding you'd enjoy more," my father explains. "But once we heard you say the aquarium, we knew we had to make it happen. It's the perfect way for a Dumas woman to say 'I do.'"

"It took all day to plan," Mila says.

"And the dress the mean Russian lady was supposed to make for me?" I ask.

"It's ready," Fingers says. "If *you* are."

"We're going to get married inside the aquarium?" I ask.

"You're going to get married inside the aquarium." Hannah laughs. "And we get to be mermaids!"

"But…" I'm still confused. "How did you guys even *get* here?"

"Listen," Mila says. "I never thought we needed the Bright Berry Monster jet. You know how I put up a fight over that thing. But right now, I'm very glad we have it! It's almost like that jet was waiting for this moment to prove itself worthy."

I just laugh.

"OK, then!" Fingers claps his hands. "Places, everyone. We have two hundred guests in front of the aquarium waiting on you!"

"Two hundred *what*?" Jesse exclaims.

"You'll see," my father says, taking Jesse by the arm and leading him away. "You'll see."

CHAPTER NINETEEN

Jack Dumas keeps his massive, fatherly hand firmly on my shoulder as he directs me down a long, narrow hallway. We stop in front of a closed door and Jack kinda spins me around to face him. Both massive hands are now both gripping my shoulders as he looks down at me from his superior height.

He's a big dude and I have to tilt my chin up pretty high to meet his gaze.

I feel like we're about to have a moment.

About his daughter. Or about me. Or about his wishes for her future. Or my level of commitment.

Something to make this event… I don't know. Worthy, maybe.

I proposed to Emma last summer. I didn't hide a ring in a cupcake, or drop it into a glass of champagne. I didn't have a plane write it in the sky or do it in front of a restaurant filled with people. I didn't make up a dance or recite her a poem. I didn't do it in front of her family.

In fact, the entire event—important as it is in the grand scheme of my life, and her life, and many other lives surrounding ours—was a small, nearly wordless moment that involved a sailboat and a stretch of sand in the middle of the water, and didn't even come with a ring.

Because I didn't know I was gonna do it.

We had taken Luke's trimaran out for an afternoon sail just after Johnny got back from his failed attempt to find Charlotte Kane. It was a warm, sunny day with clear, bright-blue skies. The water was calm and there was just a little hint of wind. We rolled out the sails after motoring a few miles west, but the wind wasn't catching them. So we just drifted, and talked, and enjoyed the sun and the break from all the crazy that comes with the last name Boston.

It was just... a nice day. A really nice day.

Emma was in a new yellow bikini she had bought the day before from her family dive shop and the way it contrasted against her long, dark hair just kinda took my breath away. She was standing on the deck gazing out at the seemingly endless horizon, dark sunglasses shading her eyes, and smiling.

That's what I remember most about that day.

Emma was smiling. Happy.

And I was thinking, *How does she do that? How does she just… live in the moment and let the stress and worry of the wider world slip away?*

Johnny came home from his trip. He brought a girl with him and she seemed cool. He seemed satisfied with her, at least. And he told us things were gonna change, but he couldn't tell us why. He told us he failed. He told us that there's a lot more to this story. And then he dropped it. Joey and I were confused, but also relieved.

Relieved that Johnny was handling things, I guess.

But the stakes were still high, the danger still real. And Emma had had no idea that I came with all this baggage. So how could she possibly be happy?

But then I thought, *Well, I'm happy. So why can't she be happy?*

Does internal satisfaction depend on external factors?

You can't ever know if you make someone happy. They can tell you with words or you can assume that you do, but you can't ever really know what's going on inside someone else's head.

But in that moment, I *knew*.

I knew the meaning of happy.

Happiness comes from being right where you're supposed to be. Happiness comes from that feeling of total acceptance and belonging. Happiness is a moment. It doesn't come with a guarantee. There's no promise of more to come, it just is.

And every moment of every day you get to choose to feel it or not.

I said, "Hey. You wanna swim out to that sandbar with me?" And I nodded my head in the general direction of a thin stretch of white sand surrounded by a swaying ocean of hidden life.

She turned, slowly, still smiling. Didn't say a word. Didn't say yes, didn't say no. Just slid her sunglasses down her face, tossed them onto a nearby table, climbed up on the railing of the side deck, and dove straight into the water.

That's when I realized something.

That's when the meaning of happy hit me.

Emma Dumas is my happy.

I climbed up on the rail and dove in after her. She was floating on her back, just smiling up at the sky as she drifted in the middle of this massive body of water. A tiny speck in a universe of everything.

So small. But so big too. Because she was my everything.

We swam out, dragged ourselves out of the heavy water and collapsed onto the sandbar. My arm was underneath her and her head was resting on my shoulder. Our feet were still in the surf and every ten seconds or so, a wave would crash over our knees and remind us to be happy.

Remind us to cherish the moments.

We stayed like that for a long while. Saying nothing. Doing nothing.

And then I took a deep breath and I said, "You're my happy, Emma. We could be drifting in the middle of nothingness and as long as you were there, I'd be happy."

She propped herself up on one elbow and looked down into my eyes. She leaned down, kissed me on the mouth, and whispered, "Yes." Then she placed one flat hand on my cheek and kissed me again.

We lingered in that kiss for many lifetimes. All of it suddenly became clear.

We were in love and we were getting married.

There was a more formal announcement later that evening in front of our family and friends and that was perfect too.

All our people in this one place, for this short

interlude of time. Something between then and now.

And it seemed… right.

"Jesse," Jack Dumas says, as he looks down at me.

"Yes, sir?"

"I'm handing her over to you now."

"I understand, sir."

"And I know you… maybe didn't have the best role model growing up. But I see a good man inside you, Jesse."

"Thank you, sir."

"And I'd just like you to know that you're one of us now. We're on the same side, son."

I nod, kind of understanding, but not really getting the specifics of that declaration. Wanting to ask more questions. But then he pushes on the door, swinging it open, and on the other side is Johnny, and Joey, and Zach.

I walk forward, momentarily forgetting about Jack Dumas.

Because these three men—these three fucked-up, dangerous, rich, powerful, weak, imperfect men… they were what was missing from this day.

They look at me and I look at them.

And just like that day I proposed to Emma, we don't need a lot of words to understand what this moment is.

It's just... happy.

Johnny nods at me. Joey starts taking off my tie. And Zach is slipping my fancy coattail jacket down my arms.

"Shirtless," Joey says. "Mermen get married shirtless."

Zach slides a chair up behind me and Johnny pushes me into it

"And barefoot," Joey adds, as Zach starts taking off my shoes and socks.

I laugh and then suddenly that dream I had the day after Emma gave me the one-up dream date comes flashing back into my head.

We were all mer-people. Emma and me. Alonzo and Johnny. Tony and Joey. Luke and Zach. Jack and Silvia. And there was Saturday night dinner. And dolphins who might've been dogs.

And that's when I know that no matter what happens after this wedding is finally over, this day is perfect because we're all here.

Together.

Johnny leans down and grabs me by the shoulders,

much the same way that Jack did. He looks straight into my eyes. "He would be proud of you, Jesse. I think you should know that. He wasn't the greatest father, but I really believe he did his best with us."

I swallow hard and nod, suddenly overcome with emotion. Suddenly overcome with love for these brothers of mine. Because yeah. Johnny might be my only true brother in this room, but the four of us... we are the definition of brotherhood.

It took a while to get here. There were many moments of silence. Many times when we were small specks floating in a huge ocean. Separate and on our own paths.

But we were never alone.

We have *never* been alone.

"This isn't a second chance," Johnny continues. "This marriage isn't some way to make up for what you think you didn't have. We don't need a do-over. You understand me, Baby Boston? We're allowed to be this way. There is no wrong or right way to love each other." He straightens up and looks at Joey, then Zach, then me. "We're *allowed* to be this way."

And that moment is back.

The silent one.

The lingering one.

The *happy* one.

"Awww, man," Zach says, pulling me to my feet and then wrapping his arms around me in a tight bear hug. "I love you, Jesse. And I want you to know that I understood what you did for me." He pulls back, wiping a tear from his eye. "You're the best brother a guy could ever ask for. And I didn't even have to ask. You just... showed up."

Joey reaches for me, putting his arms around me. He hugs me tight for several moments too long, saying nothing. Because nothing needs to be said.

We're brothers.

That's all we need to know.

Joey sucks in a deep breath as he releases me from his embrace. And then we're all looking at each other.

Happy.

When my brothers walk me out to the backstage area of the aquarium, the safety officers attach weights to my legs to make it easier to stand in the tank.

I go in the water first. They lower me on one of the mermaid swings and I stand with my bare feet on the sandy bottom of the huge tank, breathing through a hose attached to a regulator, nervous and excited that this time, for sure, is our real wedding.

I know this because on the other side of the glass, everyone is here.

Mila's husband and kids. Hannah's boyfriend, Darrel. Natalie's boy toys from the Christmas party the other night. I guess guy number two is gonna give this thing a shot? Maybe? He showed, at least. Gotta give him points for that.

Megan and Johnny are out there. He's got his arms protectively around her middle. And Joey is surrounded by his... God, what do I call that group? A posse? Partners? Lovers? Doesn't matter, I guess. They're all here. For me or him, either way, I'll take it.

And the Dumas family. Silvia is right up front waving a sign that says, *Welcome to the family, Jesse!* Which is super cute, but then again, that woman defines the word cute. Alonzo is doing that I'm-watching-you gesture with two fingers pointing to his eyes, then me.

Whatever, Lonz. You do you, dude.

Tony has his arms crossed, studying me from the other side of the glass. I'm not sure what to make of him, but I'm sure we'll make it work. Eventually.

And Luke... Luke is pressing his open mouth against the glass, wiggling his tongue at me.

What the fuck? Freak.

But then I realize he's actually doing that to Zach, who is standing next to me, also barefoot and shirtless, as my best man.

A splash from above me makes me look up and I see Hannah slipping into the water. Natalie and Mila enter next and then…

The swing lowers and there's Emma and her father descending together.

He jumps in first, then helps his daughter into the water.

Her dress isn't the one she came here in. It's the one she designed this morning. Slim and form-fitting. Hugging all her deliciously sexy curves and specially weighted so it looks pretty in the water.

Jack Dumas kisses his daughter on the cheek before they both reach for their air hoses, and then they settle to the bottom. He takes her hand, turns, and offers it to me.

Fucking Jack Dumas. I shake my head and smile. Gonna walk that only daughter of his down the aisle even if there's no aisle and it involves getting into a tank of water fully dressed in a tux.

I take Emma's hand and help her float up next to me.

Then I have a moment of panic. Who will officiate? How are we gonna do this? We don't have rings!

Then I can hear the faint sound of talking through a speaker. The ceremony is being held outside the tank, obviously. For the guests.

But you know what?

We don't need the ceremony. We've done this four times today. We're good.

And it's kinda fitting that our marriage begins in this subdued, nearly silent, underwater world.

Because who needs words when you have happy?

I take the air regulator out of my mouth and toss it aside, then take Emma's from her mouth too.

And I kiss her.

For the first time today, I kiss the bride.

CHAPTER TWENTY

The details that happen after Jesse kisses me don't really matter. It's all the usual stuff. Zach opens his hand to reveal a set of wedding rings. Jesse puts on mine, and I his. I toss a bouquet of peach water lilies and yellow water poppies. Well, toss probably isn't the right word. It kinda floats off about a foot, and then there's a flurry of mermaid tails as Natalie and Hannah make a mad dash to "catch" it.

Natalie wins. She's always been a cutthroat competitor. And she waves it around, blowing bubbles like crazy.

Then we get out of the tank and change into new clothes. Karen picked out a reception dress—and I have to admit, it's kinda pretty. A short, yellow sundress that shows off my almost perpetual tan now that Jesse and I have been spending nearly every weekend in Key West.

My hair is blow-dried and left loose. My make-up is applied by the same professional team from the Shotgun Wedding and I come to the conclusion that Karen isn't a kraken after all. I might even have to like her after all this effort she put into me and my happiness. She brought her whole family to Vegas for the wedding. Turns out Chauncey and Chance are about the same age as Mila's kids, Donny and Stephanie. They spent the entire day at the resort pool.

All the Fingers' Fantasy Wedding people are there too. The rollercoaster couple even ditched their regularly scheduled reception plans to be a part of this. The entire cast of the Treasure Island battle comes dressed as pirates and entertains the guests. Sven and his skydiving crew are drinking at the bar with my brothers, and both the bride's and groom's families from the Shotgun Wedding come still dressed in their wedding-day finery.

It's… pretty fucking perfect.

Even if I didn't plan a single moment of it.

I watch my bossy mother from across the room. She's dancing with my father. They are the most adorable couple even though my father towers over her. She's resting her head against his chest, eyes closed, smiling like this is the best day of her life.

And me?

Well, I'm slow-dancing with my new husband. Jesse is dressed in tan linen pants and a white linen button-down shirt that's mostly not buttoned, showing off his spectacular tanned chest muscles.

We're exhausted, and sore, and excited, and happy, and ready to get the fuck out of here and be alone.

Miles and Christopher are already waiting for us on the little jet. We're spending our wedding night in the jet bedroom as we fly home for Christmas day. Everyone else is taking the Bright Berry Monster.

But we're not going where Jesse *thinks* we're going.

My mother isn't the only Dumas woman who can plan a surprise.

CHAPTER TWENTY-ONE

I walk my bride backwards as we enter the jet. And when we get inside the jet bedroom, I wink at Miles and pull the pocket doors closed.

"Finally," I say, laughing as I kiss her mouth.

Her knees hit the edge of the mattress and she falls back onto the bed. And then I just... look at her. In that bright yellow sun dress. She put her hair up in pig tails on the way over here. Even though thirteen years have passed since that first day I saw her in Mallory Square, it feels like we've been together the whole time.

Hell, it feels like we've lived a lifetime in the past twenty-four hours.

"Mrs. Boston," I whisper. "You are my *jam*."

She giggles and sits up. Then in a flurry of movement, she's got her dress over her head and tosses it off to the side. She grabs my shirt and pulls me onto the bed with her. I crawl up her legs and she slowly lies back until her head hits the pillow. She's still holding my shirt with tight fists. Like she never wants to let me go.

I never want her to let me go.

But she has more in mind than just keeping me prisoner in her tight grip. Because one hand deftly pops the button on my pants and slides down inside, holding me in her palm.

I close my eyes, reminding myself to enjoy each moment.

But then she's sliding my pants and briefs over my hips, and I'm kicking off my shoes. I brace myself over her with one hand and use the other one to reach back and pull my shirt over my head.

That goes flying and then we're skin on skin, the heat of our stomachs melding together as I kick off the rest of my clothes and kiss her lips.

There's a version of this night that starts with dirty talk, a bunch of "Fuck me nows" and "I want your big, hard cock inside mes." A version where lust takes over and we get lost in the heat of the moment. A version where this is filthy, hot, sweaty sex. A version where I fuck her face and come in her throat.

And yeah. All that sounds pretty good.

Tomorrow.

But tonight… nah. I don't want to get lost in the lust or lose myself in the moment.

I want to *savor* this woman.

I ease over until I'm resting on my side, pulling down her bra so I can put her nipple in my mouth. I kiss and nip it as my fingers slip underneath the waistband of her pretty panties and begin pulling them over her hips. She lifts her legs up, bends her knees, and those panties come off without any real effort. I toss them away, then pop the clasp of her strapless bra and it falls to the side. My tongue is busy swirling around her nipple while my other hand grabs her breast firmly and squeezes.

Her hand is back on my cock, slowly sliding up and down my shaft. This slowness, it's almost agonizing. And when the tip of her thumb begins caressing the tip of my cock head, I have to close my eyes and remember to breathe. She feels *that* good.

Her fingers reach down and play with my balls as I slide my hand down her stomach, over her hip bone, and slip it right between her legs. I press two fingers inside her wet opening and she arches her back a little. And when I glance up at her face, she's got her eyes closed and she's biting her lip.

I want to wait. I want to explore her body and play with her pussy forever.

But she takes that decision away from me when she maneuvers her legs over me and takes over, becoming the bossy bride she was always meant to be.

She rubs her pussy over the top of my cock as she holds my face in her hands and kisses my lips. Then she reaches down with one hand, slips my cock inside her, and begins to move.

It's a slow rocking motion. And her breasts slide up and down my chest as she sinks down on my cock.

I give up. Hell, I give up. I smile and let her have her way.

No words are said as we make love.

They're just not necessary.

Time passes, or it doesn't.

Memories are made or maybe remembered.

Love is long and lasts for moments that drag on forever.

Happiness is found and all our mistakes are forgiven.

When I wake up, I'm alone and Miles is standing over my naked body holding a sterling silver tray in one hand and matching silver tongs gripping a small white towel in the other.

And somehow… this seems right.

I chuckle and stare up at him through one half-cracked eye. "Miles, my man. What's up?"

"I have a lemon-scented hot towel for you, sir."

I point at him. "You're even cooler today than you were yesterday, you know that, Miles?"

"I do, sir."

"Hey!" I sit up. "What happened at the poker game?"

"I didn't play, sir. I helped the Kraken plan the wedding."

"Aww, shit. I'm sorry."

"No need to be sorry, sir. It was my pleasure. And exceeding expectations is part of my job description."

"But the trip was my Christmas present to you." I swing my legs over the side of the bed, grab the towel and wipe my face with it, then look up at him. "Now I'll have to think of something else."

"I have a request, sir. If you're strapped for ideas."

"Hit me, Miles. I'm all ears. I can't fuckin' wait to hear your request." I peek at the spread on the silver tray, then take a small bowl of Barbie and Ken rolls and pour them into my mouth, chewing thoughtfully as I try to imagine what kind of present Miles would be interested in. A nice watch? A new suit? A crazy Vegas wedding for himself and Christopher?

"I would like you to kill someone."

I spit out the half-chewed cinnamon rolls and start coughing. He slaps me on the back and gives me a minute.

"What?" I finally manage to croak.

"Kidding." He flashes half a smile. "We both know you're not the killer in the family."

I point at him again. "You're a dick, you know that, Miles?"

"I do, sir."

"Seriously, what do you want for your present? I'm kinda rich, so don't be shy. But I'm not gonna kill anyone. I really don't have it in me."

"Of course not, sir. I would like for you to help out Mr. Dumas. He's in a spot."

"Jack?"

"No, sir. Alonzo. He's in some trouble and requires assistance. But he won't ask. He can't tell Tony what he's been up to because he will never hear the end of it, his father is busy with other things, Luke is in the middle of a blissful sexual threesome, Johnny doesn't like him, and while Joey did build his current life on a bed of lies, he's not really the man for the job. So that leaves you."

"Wait." I put up a hand. "What the fuck are you talking about? What job?"

"Alonzo, sir. He's having… girl trouble."

I bark out a laugh so loud, Miles takes a step back. "Alonzo needs my help with a *girl?*"

"He does, sir. When I signed on to work for Miss Dumas, now Mrs. Boston, I signed on to take care of her whole family. And I have noticed that Alonzo is struggling in the love department. He has trouble opening up and I feel like you have mastered this particular skill. At the very least you are the first to make it official." He stops and smiles.

I wait for more info, but he seems to have finished his little speech.

I let out a long breath. "Miles?"

"Yes, sir?"

"I feel like you're not quite grasping the meaning of the word 'present.' When a billionaire offers you the gift of your choice you ask for… I dunno. A fancy car, or a racehorse, or hell, a Fabergé egg, if that's your thing. You do not ask him to give his brother-in-law love lessons."

"I understand, sir."

"OK." I nod "OK. Then… what kind of present do you want?"

"I would like you to give Alonzo love lessons, sir."

"No, Miles! My man. That's not—"

"Knock, knock!" The pocket door is sliding open

as these words come out of Emma's mouth. "You awake, Mr. Boston?"

"Hey, Mrs. Boston," I say, smiling up at my wife. "I'm up."

She glances down at my morning wood and chuckles. "I can see that. But Christopher tells me we're about to land, so get dressed. It's Christmas! And I have a very, very special present planned for you." She waggles her eyebrows at me.

"Oh!" I laugh. "OK, then! I'll be right out."

She closes the door and I turn back to Miles. "Miles, don't ask me to do this. That dude hates my guts. Like, he seriously planned the skydiving hoping I'd die. Or at the very least be seriously injured. I'm really not the man for the job."

"Yes, sir."

"Great. So what can I get you?"

"Love lessons for Alonzo, sir."

I throw up my hands. "That's not how you play!"

"I know, sir. You're the expert. That's why Alonzo needs you."

"How do you even know he needs me?"

"I spy on him, sir."

"Wait, what?"

"I spy on all of you, sir. My organization is... equipped for such things."

"What *organization*?"

"Jesse!" Emma calls from the middle cabin. "We're landing!"

"Coming!" I stand up and start pulling on my pants, then direct my attention back to Miles. "Like... the Worldwide Butlers' Club?"

"Precisely, sir."

"That was a joke, Miles. Who do you work for?"

"Jesse!"

"Jesus Christ, Emma. I'm coming!" I point at Miles. "We're not done here."

"We are, sir. I'll forward you all my info via email. Merry Christmas." Then he walks to the door, opens it up, and slides it closed behind him.

I let out a long breath. Alonzo?

Nope. I'm gonna go buy Miles a nice watch and call it good.

I find my shirt and shoes, finish getting dressed, and then join Emma at the breakfast table just as we begin our descent.

"Quick," she says, pointing to the table. "Eat. Because once we land, we have things to do."

"What things?" I ask, grabbing a piece of toast and shoving it in my mouth. "What does the Dumas family do on Christmas Day? Oh, do we get to have a make-up dinner because we missed last night? God, I hope so. I'm starving."

"Mmmm… no," Emma says, shrugging her shoulders up to her ears as she grins big.

"Sailing? Diving? Water-skiing? What else do you guys do? Oh, I know—fishing. Are we going fishing?"

"Nope." She's still grinning like a mad woman.

"Then why are we in a hurry?" I look down at the breakfast. I could eat this whole table, that's how hungry I am.

"You'll see." And just as she says that, the jet lands and we brake hard. "But I'm gonna need you to put these on."

I glance at the headphones Emma is offering me. "What?"

"Just put them on. And this too." She opens one closed fist to reveal a blindfold.

"Mrs. Boston," I say.

"Mr. Boston?"

"What the hell are you up to?"

"You'll see. Just put them on. Trust me, you don't want to ruin this surprise."

"It's a Christmas present?"

"Yes, it's a Christmas present." She shakes the headphones at me.

"Is it a Lamborghini?"

"No." She chuckles. "We already have one of

those."

"Hmm. Is it… a sex toy?"

"Jesse Boston!"

"What? That's what people use headphones and blindfolds for, right?"

She gets up out of her seat, even though we're still taxiing, and walks around the table, slips the blindfold over my eyes, and slaps the headphones over my ears. Then she pulls one away from my ear, leans into me, and whispers, "Do not even think about peeking, mister."

"Bossy," I say.

She lets the headphone slap back against my head and music starts to play. Classical music with the volume turned way, way up. So I literally cannot hear a damn thing.

Once the jet has stopped, she leads me out. It's a little chilly this morning in Key West, and I suddenly hope we're not going diving. I hate being in the water when it's cold.

Emma leads me by the arm. I try to pay attention. Try to figure out where we're at. I'm pretty familiar with the Key West airport. We fly in to the jet club a lot. But I can't, for the life of me, figure out exactly where we are in the club without eyes and ears.

She's probably taking me to the marina. I bet

there's a yacht involved. Maybe she didn't buy me one, but she knows how much I love sailing.

Or maybe we're going back to her parents' house for a huge reception. I can see Emma wanting total control over the wedding reception since her bossy mom and Kraken Karen actually did get their way in all things Baby Boston wedding.

Or maybe... she's taking me to a five-star hotel and when she takes this blindfold off, she'll be standing there in kinky lingerie, ready for another wedding night?

I like all these ideas as she puts a hand on my head, indicating I should duck and get into the waiting car. I'm actually pretty excited about this little surprise she's cooked up.

Then the car is moving. But... the drive is kinda long. And there's a lot of traffic because it feels like every minute or so we stop to wait at a light.

Where the hell are we?

Finally we stop and I'm helped out of the car. Emma's hand finds mine and we're walking again. Definitely outside. And it's not Key West. I know this for sure now. It's cold.

But pretty soon we're inside again. Then we're on an elevator.

I think I've been a good sport so far, but now I'm

dying! Like… dying to know what the hell is happening. Because it's Christmas and if we're not in Key West—holy shit. My new mother-in-law is gonna kill me if we don't show up for Christmas.

Missing Christmas Eve for a crazy wedding she planned? Yeah, New Mom is all over that. On board, as they say. But missing *the day?*

Nah. I'm dead. I'm so dead when we get back in Key West.

Then we stop. I reach for my blindfold, convinced it's time. But Emma's hand stops me. Then she lifts one headphone away from my ear and says, "OK. We're here. Are you ready for your Christmas present, husband of mine?"

I grin like a kid. "So ready. Hit me, Emma. Hit me with your best shot."

She giggles. "I'm starting to think you have a thing for Pat Benatar."

"I have a thing for you."

"OK. Here we go." She lifts the headphones off my head, then whispers, "Take off your blindfold."

For a moment I'm super nervous and I hesitate. Because something about this place feels… familiar. And then… I know.

I know where we are.

I lift the blindfold up and off, holding it tight in my

hand.

And I just look around in wonder.

A massive Christmas tree is in front of the window that has too many panes of glass. So many it looks like a checkerboard. Underneath are mounds of presents, some wrapped for Christmas, some for a wedding reception. And right next to it is the Santa Machine.

The entire dining room is filled with food. Turkey, and ham, and a seven-tier wedding cake. There is a roaring fire in the fireplace and hanging from the mantle are stockings.

A lot of stockings and these stockings have names.

But the names I really pay attention to are written in little-boy cursive with red glitter glue.

Then I look at Johnny and shake my head. "What's going on?"

I know what's going on. I just don't understand it. We're in the Bossy Building. Up on the family floor. The whole place is decked out for Christmas. Like... I'm starting to think Joey or Johnny ripped off a department store, that's how huge this Christmas display is.

Johnny lets go of Megan's hand and walks across the living room, his puppy, Jasper, trotting at his heels. It's a massive room, filled with couches and chairs arranged into many mini-seating areas. And as he crosses, he passes many people.

All the people.

All *my* people.

The whole Dumas family. Silvia, Jack, Alonzo, Tony, and Luke.

The whole Boston family. Zach, and Joey, and Brooke, and Huck, and Wald, and even Maisy, and Malinda, and Michael Conner are here.

And Mila. And Diego. And Stephanie and Donny. And Hannah and Darrel.

Even Natalie and her two boys.

Hell, even Key West Naked Girl is here, standing right between Luke and Zach. Everyone is here.

Johnny finally reaches me. He places both hands on my shoulders, just like he did last night. And he looks right into my eyes. "I know what I said last night. We are allowed to love each other any way we want. And we don't need"—he pans his hand at the room and all it contains—"we don't need all *this* to show that love. But you know what, brother?"

"What?" I whisper, searching his eyes for the answer.

"It's time we let go of what we missed out on and embrace what we have."

And that's when I realize something.

I knew that already.

CHAPTER TWENTY-TWO

EMMA

There's a long moment of silence when I fear that I've overstepped. Jesse left this place. He left the Bossy Building behind and he said he never wanted to go back. All four of these Boston boys left this place and never wanted to come back.

But... why? Why walk away from your home just because that home looks nothing like it should? Why give up on who you are just because it's hard to define and even harder to understand?

I have been planning this for weeks now. It took me several conversations to get Johnny and Joey on board. But Zach was my ally. Zach was the only way this Christmas present happened. He talked to them for me. He convinced them that this was a good thing and Jesse—hell, all of them—deserve to be here. This is their home. Good or bad, like it or not, this is where they grew up. Nothing can ever change that.

"But you know what can change?" Zach told them. "Us. *We* can change. We can look for the good in our past instead of the bad. And we can start doing that this year by picking up where we left off and making it better. Even though there's never been a Christmas tradition at the Bossy, there can be now."

I was so sure this was the right move.

And then Jesse told me how sad this place made him and I second-guessed.

But by Christmas Eve, it was too late. I had already convinced my parents and brothers that we needed to be here, not down in Key West, for Christmas Day. I had already put my foot down and told them we needed to share this holiday from now on. And even though everyone grumbled about it right up to Christmas week, after that wedding they planned for me, they knew they had to do this.

Maybe Alonzo isn't here for Jesse, but he is here for me.

Then I had to convince Mila, Hannah, and Natalie that we're a family and they had to come too. So they rearranged their holiday—twice, actually. Since I bossed them into this party at the Bossy and my mother bossed them into the wedding in Vegas.

It was a lot of work but it felt right.

It still feels right.

But will Jesse agree?

Johnny withdraws his hands from Jesse's shoulders and I bite my lip, waiting for Jesse's reaction. And when he looks at me I say, "Surprise!" in a small, unsure voice.

He takes a deep, deep breath. Then he smiles and points his finger at me. "Well, played, Mrs. Boston. Well played."

I let out a nervous laugh. "Yeah?"

"Yeah. But"—he holds up his hand—"you're not gonna win this one, you know."

"Win? What?"

"The one-up Christmas game. Because lady…" He steps forward towards me, turns and places both his hands on my cheeks, and kisses me. And in this kiss he whispers, "I got you a present money can't buy."

I giggle into our kiss. "What's that, Mr. Boston?"

He takes a step back and snaps his fingers. Then Joey is in motion. He darts over to the tree, fishes around for a present, and holds it up like a prize. "Got it!" He beams a smile at me as he hurries over to Jesse to hand it to him.

Jesse takes it. It's a beautifully wrapped gift. I can't figure out if it's a wedding gift or a Christmas gift. The paper is silver with blue bells on it and that could go either way.

Jesse holds it up. "Emma, I only have one regret. Just one. I wish I could've been there for the thirteen years I missed with you. And I wish you could've been there for the thirteen years you missed with me. So I made you this."

"Actually," Huck says, holding up a finger, "this was my idea."

"Shut up, Huck," Jesse growls.

Huck puts up surrender hands. "I'm just saying."

Jesse glares at him. But then he says, "We"—as he looks around the room at our family and friends—"*we* did this. For you. And me too. So… I hope you like it."

He hands me the gift, which is about the size of a shirt box you'd get from a department store.

"But you have to sit down," Maisy says, pulling on my hand and leading me to the couch where my parents are sitting. They move over and make room for Jesse and me. And now I'm like… super excited. What could possibly be in this box that could win the one-up game? I mean, this Bossy surprise is pretty fuckin' fantastic. This is my yacht on the one-up dream date. This is the moment that Jesse realized I was the boss.

We sit down between my parents and everyone in the room starts rearranging chairs or sitting on tables, so they can see the present when I open it.

Then it all happens at once. I pull the blue satin ribbon off the present, lift the lid off the box, and push the tissue paper out of the way.

Inside is a photo album. And on the front it says, *My Life with You, Uninterrupted.*

I open it and right from the first page I know.

I know.

He won.

Because this is a picture of me at my high school prom. But I'm not with that date my mother bossed me into going with.

I'm with Jesse Boston.

"What the hell?" I laugh.

And then the whole story of the photo album comes spilling out of Joey's mouth, Huck interrupting at regular intervals, Wald adding his two cents. They explain how they needed to fake out Michael Conner to get custody of Maisy and how they hired people all over the world to fake social media pictures of them. And how Jesse wanted so badly to get a second chance with me, he asked if they could make a fantasy life. One where we were never apart.

My mother gave him baby pictures of me. And even though Jesse only has one single picture of him as a baby and his face is Photoshopped—badly, in most of them—onto every single one of me during my toddler years, I don't care. In one, we're in a little plastic pool together as infants. And we celebrate our birthdays together. All the birthdays. Someone used age-progression on Jesse's baby picture, you can tell. But some of them are real and even Jesse is surprised when he sees these.

And prom night, of course. And pictures of me standing next to Jesse for every one of his yacht wins. And pictures of Jesse standing next to me, Mila, Hannah, and Natalie as we opened our first cosmetics shop. When we got our awards. There's even fake magazine interviews with our faces on the covers.

And even though I know every bit of this is fake, I believe it.

And Jesse… well, Jesse just grins like a man who just won a thirteen-year do-over.

"But wait," Tony says, forcing our father to move aside so he can squeeze in. "You're missing the best part." He flips the book to the back and reveals a whole section of pictures that are not Photoshopped.

Because they had people photographing us for every single moment of our fantasy wedding day.

Jesse tasting wedding cake.

Me choosing a dress from the roller-skating fashion show.

Our screaming faces on the roller coaster.

Jesse swinging from the ropes on the pirate ship.

Our combined terror and excitement during the skydive.

The huge Italian wedding.

A picture of the ass-end-of-wedding-day getaway car, tin cans trailing behind us.

They even have a pic of our kidnapping!

And, of course, the real wedding at the aquarium.

I am stunned into silence as I look at all the memories we've collected.

Jesse leans in next to me and whispers in my ear. "This is just the beginning, Mrs. Boston. You haven't seen anything yet."

I lean back into the seat cushions, Tony on my right and Jesse on my left.

And I sigh.

Because even though it's a fantasy, it's still real.

I win.

That's all there is to it.

But Emma did have another present for me inside the Santa Machine. She waited until all the festivities were over before she told me that. We opened up all the presents. We ate a huge dinner. Hell, we even watched *Home Alone*, which I had never bothered to watch before, but I totally relate to Kevin. And then, once all the locals went home and the Dumas family was tucked up tight on the Jesse and Joey floors, she took me over to the Santa Machine and handed me a lanyard with my name on it.

"Go on," she said. "Scan it."

And look, I'm not gonna play this cool. I was freaking excited about the Santa Machine. She did not have to tell me twice. So I scanned.

And then I got an email notification on my phone. A letter from Santa!

And this is what it said:

Dear Jesse,

Santa Machine hears that you've been a very good boy this year. So Emma Elf wanted me to present you with the Emma's Fantasy Christmas Pick Three Buffet.

But there's a catch, of course. You don't get to choose. She chooses for you.

I hope you're ready.
Merry Christmas.

Love, Santa Machine and Emma Elf

And do you know what she chose for me?

Well, let me just say we live in the Bossy Building now. Family floor. That was number one and even though I was worried that Chek would object, since he's the money-maker now, he was pretty cool about it. Anyway, he lives three floors up on Johnny's old level, so we never even see him. I feel like the whole Bossy thing is gonna work itself out. Because if Johnny was worried about it, he would not have helped us move all our shit from Emma's apartment. And he did. So. I kinda love living at the Bossy again now that Emma's here to share it with me.

Unconventional as it is, I can't deny that the Bossy is my true home.

Of course, you can't call yourself Emma Elf and

not show up for bed that night wearing a sexy elf costume. So that was fun. I made her ears blush with all the filthy hot things my tongue did to her that night.

But the third... well, let's just say in seven months Zach will be the only Boston brother without a kid.

Yeah.

I know what Johnny said. I get it. We don't need a do-over.

But if you get one, man... you gotta grab onto that shit with all you've got and never let go.

And that's exactly what I plan to do.

Never let go.

Welcome to the End of Book Shit. I'm sure you know the drill already since this is book four in a series but I always like to explain this when I write one of these because sometimes they have typos (I don't edit them) and sometimes they are rambling rants. So the EOBS is where I get to say anything I want about the story you just read.

Well, the first thing I have to say is that I'M SO GLAD I GOT TO WRITE ANOTHER BOOK ABOUT EMMA AND JESSE!!! I thought Bossy Jesse was a pretty fun book. These two have some serious chemistry and that was perfect for a second-chance enemies-to-lovers romance, right! I loved their banter

313

in the first book and it was mostly just a fun book. But of course I'm not really known for my fun books I'm known for the mind-fuck books. So I fucked your mind a little at the end.

Then Joey's book was more about a guy and a girl trying to figure out who they were (and as part of a foursome, no less. That's not easy.) And Johnny's book was all about him really coming to terms with his limitations. When to fold and when to hold, so to speak. He didn't fold. Not really. I think his book was more of a second chance too, just with himself and not with his love interest, Megan.

So this book—I knew this book was gonna be fun because Jesse and Emma are just fun people. And I really wanted them to have a crazy adventure together on the way to the altar. And what better place to have a crazy wedding adventure than Vegas!

But I also wanted to include all her girls, and all the boys, and get a glimpse of Key West one more time before going on this journey. The Dumas brothers are up next, starting with Alonzo, so they needed some page time.

And I needed for everyone to be there for the final wedding because the Dumas family is all about 'family'. And even though Jesse probably thought he didn't need his family there, he realized he did. And the final wedding, though far from perfect and certainly not anything close to a 'dream wedding', really was kinda perfect when you look at these people as a whole.

Aquarium, mermaids, shirtless Jesse, and wet-wedding-dress Emma. She was a good sport, wasn't she? Lol I felt sorry for Emma quite a few times throughout this story. That's why I gave her some girl-time for the Shotgun Wedding.

By the way, all these wedding can be done in Vegas. Maybe not exactly how I wrote them—but if you've got a guy called Fingers arranging it, I'm sure he'd pull through for you too.

One other interesting thing that's kinda fun. Shoes is a real guy. My Uncle Bill, in fact. I didn't know a Fingers, but there was a "Fingers Figure" in the picture when I was a kid. Because my Uncle Bill really did play cards with the mob— in my aunt's dining room, no less. And there really was a Freddie's Pizza in Pittsburgh. My aunt and uncle lived just down the road from Freddie's II. So Shoes was my uncle. He was a weird dude. He took me places like the racetrack, football games, and yeah, card games. But I wasn't allowed IN the card games. Not because I was a kid, but because I was a *girl*. I won't go into details about the stories I have about being his niece, but it was... *interesting*.

There's always something true in my stories. Always.

I spent a lot time trying to think up what kind of presents Jesse and Emma could get each other for Christmas because what the hell do you buy someone who can buy themselves anything they want? At this kind of wealth presents stop being about things and they become about the thought. It really is the thought that counts. For all presents, actually.

I knew Emma's present to Jesse – Christmas at the Bossy. And this was because her family was so tight, and his family was so loose, it never really occurred to her that Jesse wouldn't want a family Christmas. But of course it all worked out in the end.

But it took me a long time to come up with Jesse's present to Emma. I think I was more than half-way through the book when I finally figured out he wanted to give her more memories. It was the perfect gift for Emma. The perfect way to make-up for time lost. And that present would've been fine. Great. It was a very fun, cool, heartfelt present all on its own. But then I realized that their wedding was jam-packed full of memories. So in the end, the fake memories were still fun, but totally unnecessary.

And while this is a Christmas book – pretty much all of it happens on Christmas Eve—it's really more of a wedding book. That's what I was aiming for. I wanted it to be cool, fun wedding book like Mr. & Mrs. was for the Misters series. Of course, there was only one couple getting married in this book. I'm not sure there's a wedding in Joey, Brooke, Huck, and Wald's future. How's that work, right? So far plural marriages are still illegal. So the wedding book for Joey et el will have to wait. Or maybe they never get married? I know romance readers love the wedding, but they aren't really an indicator of a happily ever after. And Johnny and Megan... I'm not sure what will happen after their one year is up. She's pregnant, so directive number one for the Way has been met. But... now what?

We'll have to see. I think that story will start coming back around in Tony's book. No date on that yet, but Alonzo will release in January 2020. I have two books that are not Bossy before Tony's book releases, so Tony's book will probably be in April, I guess. By the way – I am apologizing ahead of time for naming one of Emma's brothers TONY. Because if you read the Company books you know we HAD a Tony already. But I forgot I had used that name before. So- if this confused you (and it might after you read Creeping Beautiful because I use a name a second time in that one on purpose) then I'm sorry! I totally just forgot there was another Tony and there is no hidden

317

meaning behind this, I just made a mistake. :)

Also, before I forget, there's a few crossover/call-backs in this book. One is "the hazmat girl" Indie is her name, from Johnny's book. And Chek, also from Johnny's book. And Wendy. Chek's daughter. You'll meet Wendy for real in Creeping Beautiful, which releases in February 2020.

Last year I stopped writing standalones about mid-year and when I started the Bossy series I knew it was gonna loop around to the Company, but I wasn't sure I would mention the Company name. Well, I did that in Johnny's book. And if you read Creeping Beautiful, you'll see a bunch of new characters, but also a bunch of old characters too.

The Bossy Brothers are Company.

I didn't start the Tragic book with this kind of cross-connection in mind, but by the time I got to Ford's book, I was already knew deep in the weeds with Sasha Cherlin. She drove me into this crazy world of the Company, The Way, The Silver Society (From the Misters) and she's still popping up in Creeping Beautiful in 2020, even though her books started back in 2014.

And… for the record. I'm loving all the connections in Bossy Brothers. It took me a couple years after finishing up Five to find a new entry point, but for me it was worth the wait. And if you're a Company fan, then I can't wait for you to discover all the little crossovers in Creeping Beautiful. This book is about the other side of the Company. Not the ones who took it down—the ones who got left behind.

OK, that's it for me. I hope you had fun running around Vegas getting married with Jesse and Emma. I sure did. And I hope you keep going with Alonzo because his story is FUN too. Not a big mystery like Johnny. But don't worry, there is mystery in there. And Alonzo isn't nearly as uptight as he comes off from the Boston perspective.

So thank you for reading, thank you for reviewing (please don't forget to leave a review for Bossy Bride at the retailer where you purchased it). And I'll see you in the next book!

Happy Holidays, my bitches. Love you.

Julie
JA Huss

JA Huss never wanted to be a writer and she still dreams of that elusive career as an astronaut. She originally went to school to become an equine veterinarian but soon figured out they keep horrible hours and decided to go to grad school instead. That Ph.D. wasn't all it was cracked up to be (and she really sucked at the whole scientist thing), so she dropped out and got a M.S. in forensic toxicology just to get the whole thing over with as soon as possible.

After graduation she got a job with the state of Colorado as their one and only hog farm inspector and spent her days wandering the Eastern Plains shooting the shit with farmers.

After a few years of that, she got bored. And since she was a homeschool mom and actually does love science, she decided to write science textbooks and make online classes for other homeschool moms.

She wrote more than two hundred of those workbooks and was the number one publisher at the online homeschool store many times, but eventually she covered every science topic she could think of and ran out of shit to say.

So in 2012 she decided to write fiction instead. That year she released her first three books and started a career that would make her a New York Times bestseller and land her on the USA Today Bestseller's List twenty-one times in the next five years.

In May 2018 MGM Television bought the TV and film rights for five of her books in the Rook & Ronin and Company series' and in March 2019 they offered her and her writing partner, Johnathan McClain, a script deal to write a pilot for a TV show.

Her books have sold millions of copies all over the world, the audio version of her semi-autobiographical book, Eighteen, was nominated for a Voice Arts Award and an Audie Award in 2016 and 2017 respectively, her audiobook, Mr. Perfect, was nominated for a Voice Arts Award in 2017, and her audiobook, Taking Turns, was nominated for an Audie Award in 2018. In 2019 her book, Total Exposure, was nominated for a Romance Writers of America RITA Award.

Johnathan McClain is her first (and only) writing partner and even though they are worlds apart in just about every way imaginable, it works.

She lives on a ranch in Central Colorado with her family.